Fort Sherwood

Fort Sherwood

A Fort Lost in Time

alvah phillips

FORT SHERWOOD
A FORT LOST IN TIME

iUniverse books may be ordered through booksellers or by contacting:

iUniverse
1663 Liberty Drive
Bloomington, IN 47403
www.iuniverse.com
844-349-9409

ISBN: 978-1-6632-4075-0 (sc)
ISBN: 978-1-6632-4076-7 (e)

Library of Congress Control Number: 2022910642

Print information available on the last page.

iUniverse rev. date: 06/07/2022

Prologue

Thomas Veer is a United States senator that has sponsored many scientific projects.

Gwen Veer Grey is the senator's daughter. She is in charge of project Camel Otter at the Fort Sherwood site in England.

Tom Planck is over project Camel Otter at Cambridge

Gen. Sam Tayler is in charge of Fort Sherwood.

Fort Sherwood and project Camel Otter are to find ways of teleportation of solid material across distances.

A. C. Phillips

1

Project Camel Otter at Cambridge

Veer was approaching Project Camel Otter, the limo was entering Cambridge, he was almost there. Veer looked at the email again. The text part read, Senator Thomas Veer, we are going to perform our first test of project Camel-Otter April 7 at ten a. m.

You are invited to attend. Invited, dam, you might say he owned the place. He nearly alone in the senate, had got the government to invest over 600 million dollars in this project. The limo had turned off Interstate 95 soon they would be on state 3 they were nearly there. Yes, there it was, to the public, the new quantum physics building. It was so much more than that. The Boston project had been used to cover up some of the rock and soil they had to get rid of. Two hundred feet below this building was a nuclear power plant. They could not pull the amount of power they needed off the grid. There were hidden pipes to the Charles River for water for the reactor. Now the driver opened the limo door and Veer started to the building. Before he was halfway there two people were walking with him. Opening doors for him, pointing the way. Then, he entered a room with a large screen and 20 comfortable chairs. Several of the scientist smiled or spoke to him. Tom Planck, the head of the project, came to him, greeted him and said, "this is a small test about one thousandth of a normal projection." "The test is being done by our unit in England, we will just be watching on the screen." The screen lit up; It was an aerial view of what appeared to be a small army base with a large earthen berm all the way around it. The berm was new, Senator Veer spoke up and said, "what is the berm for?" "Oh,"

1

Planck said, "it is just safety in case of any stray radiation." "When they created the reactor lake, they used that dirt and lead ore to build the berm." Now the screen changed. It was in the main lab with all the equipment. And there she was, his daughter, the light of his life, a beautiful double P.H.D. female. She said, "Today we are doing a small experiment, as we feel our way in uncharted territory." She started going to each console and explaining what each one did. Now she came to one operated by a doctor Phitto, and she explained his was the power control. Today he would be using less than one percent of their available power. Now she went on to another, but Veer's mind was still on Phitto, he was sweating, and no one else was sweating. Now Gwen Veer Grey (her name was from a short marriage) was showing the projection chamber that would send the test article to them. It should wind up in an identical chamber here in this building. Now Gwen started a count down from 20 and the screen went from console to console and there was Phitto pushing a large red handle all the way to the stop. Now the image on the screen became distorted and then went blank. Senator Veer was on his feet, "what the heck happened Planck?" Stammering, Planck said "I do not know, but Ronald is trying to contact them." Senator Veer, "what do you mean trying to contact them?" "They do not respond either radio or phone, they do not respond." Senator Veer red faced and flustered said, "Planck, you better find out quick what happened and if my daughter is safe. And added for your sake Planck she better be." Now Senator Veer stormed out of the building back to his waiting limo.

2

At Fort Sherwood

The large room was filled with smoke, two consoles were on fire. People were staggering, coughing, laying on the floor. lt. Marvin and two enlisted men rush in with fire extinguishers, put out the fires, and begin to help the remaining people out of the room. Some had to be taken to medical. Now that room was empty, and twenty people were in the dimly lit lobby. The only light was what came through the windows.

Lt. Marvin, "What happened."

Gen. Sam Tayler, "We do not know."

Lt. lance, "Gen. we do not have electricity."

Gen. "Lt. Marvin can you get the emergency generators going?"

Lt. Marvin, "Yes sir, right away."

Gen. to his number one, "We have to get to the reactor."

Lt. Lance, "Will the elevator work on emergency power?"

Gen. Tayler, "I don't know, we should probably use the ladder."

Lt. lance, "That is 200 feet, it is only for emergencies."

Gen. Tayler, "I know, and this is one, make sure everyone is out of the control room."

Lt. Sarah Margo, "Gen. Tayler we have no communications."

Gen. Tayler, "What do you mean?"

Lt. Margo, indignant, "Just what I said, no phones, no radio, and none of the satellites".

Tayler to Master Sargent Mills, "Sarge take a squad outside and see what is going on."

Nearly all the 377 people on the base are now in the, so called, science building, making a lot of noise and wanting information.

Lt. Gareth came to Tayler and asked, "What can I do to help?"

Tayler, "Grab some men and go to the gate, no one comes in or goes out until we figure this out."

Gen. Tayler, "Colonel Bradley, you are in charge, Lance and I have to go to the Sinkhole, (this was the code name for a secret part of the project).

Col. Bradley, "Yes sir, Gen."

Gen. Tayler and Lance are now at a steel door. Tayler punches in an eight-digit code then does a palm print, and then looks into a scanner. The door operating on backup batteries opens and Tayler and Lance enter a small room as the steel door closes behind them. There is a rack with head lamps, and both put them on. Lance walks to the ladder, it is a black hole, the only light is his headlamp. Lance climbs 50 feet down to the first platform and calls to Tayler, "O.K. I am on section 2," and they proceeded down to the reactor. This was a very secret part of the project, even the people on the base thought it was a Neutrino laboratory. The project required massive amount of power. Much more than they could pull off the English grid. The reactor crew were working with battery powered emergency lighting and a large diesel generator was already running. Its intake and exhaust were on the surface, so as not to affect the air in the lab.

Captain Nimmer to Gen. Tayler, "What the heck happened? If this is a test you should tell us first, we are running a hot reactor."

Gen. Tayler, "It was not a test, and we do not know what happened."

Now for the first time Tayler's base radio crackles, "Tayler this is Valdez."

Gen. Tayler, "Go ahead Lt. Valdez."

Lt. Valdez, "Gen. Tayler I have our base radio system operating on emergency power, but we cannot contact anybody on the outside."

Lt. Gareth, breaks in on the radio and says, "Col. you are not going to believe this."

Gen. Tayler says, "All right, tell me."

Lt. Gareth, "One hundred feet outside the berm the road ends."

Gen. Tayler, "Lt. Gareth, what do you mean?"

Lt. Gareth, "Gen. Tayler, approx. 100 to 200 feet outside the berm, all the way around we have Forrest, that is all we see."

Gen. Tayler looked at Lance and Nimmer and asked, "Any ideas". Tayler pushed the button on the radio and said, "Gareth, you and your men stay there, I will be there as soon as I can". Tayler pushed the button again; "Lt. Marvin is your bird, o.k.?"

Lt. Marvin, "Yes sir, I believe it is."

Gen. Tayler, "Get it ready to fly I will be there soon."

Captain Nimmer (nickname Nemo), "The elevator is usable now".

Back on the surface Lt. Lance heads for the gate and Gen. Tayler heads for the motor pool. He finds Lt. Marvin and two helpers at the four-seater turbine powered helicopter.

Gen. Tayler, "I want to go up." Lt. Marvin flip some switches and the rotors began to turn slowly. Now the rpm speeds up and soon Lt. Marvin motions for Tayler to join him. Now with Tayler belted in and wearing earphones, Marvin increases power, and the helicopter lifts off. Even at 100 feet they could see they were in a different world. All they could see was Forrest and open spaces. They went higher to nearly 600 ft and straining looking in all directions, the only buildings they could see were buildings both to the east and west that looked like crudely built villages. They were at the fringe of vision at least 15 miles away.

3

At Fort Sherwood

Now Gen. Tayler calls Gareth and says," There are three locals on the east side of the berm, go get them, we need to talk to them."

Lt. Gareth, "Yes sir, where do I take them?" Tayler had to think about it, where he could safely take them. The combo mess hall for everyone enlisted, scientist and officers was on the outside of the complex.

Gen. Tayler "Take them to the combo mess hall, I will meet you there."

Gen. Tayler to Marvin, "Take her down."

Lt. Marvin landed on the roll around platform in front of the motor pool.

Climbing down Gen. Tayler asked, "what kind of shape is it in?"

Lt. Marvin: "Very good sir it went through a major 6 months ago."

Gen. Tayler; "How about fuel?"

Lt. Marvin: "The bird and the emergencies run on the same fuel. The tanks capacity is 10,000 but all we have is 7500."

Gen. Tayler: "And those emergency diesels are using it right now."

Lt. Marvin; "Yes sir."

Gen. Tayler on his radio; "Sam to Captain Nimmer."

Capt. Nimmer; "Yes, go ahead."

Gen. Tayler: "Nimmer, you have a blank check, use whoever and whatever you need. I want that reactor to provide electricity for the whole base, and I want it yesterday. I will fill you in later but believe me this is extremely important."

Nimmer to Tayler, "we are cooling with the backup system."

Gen. Tayler, "what is wrong with the main system."

Nimmer, "we do not know, it uses river water."

Gen. Tayler, "Oh crap."

Nimmer, "what was that?"

Gen. Tayler, "Nothing I will talk to you later."

Lt. Marvin puzzled, "Reactor sir."

Gen. Tayler: "I do not think secrecy matters any more, that neutrino lab is really a nuclear power generator."

Lt. Marvin: "Dam, but that is good for us."

Gen. Tayler: "Yes, but we must connect it to the base grid."

Lt. Marvin; "Yes in a few days our tanks will be dry."

Gen. Tayler: "We cannot have that we have to save some for the bird, the hum v, the caterpillar, and the half- track."

Gen. Tayler on radio; "Lt. Lance can you go back down to the cellar and help Nimmer with the project?"

Lt Lance, "Yes sir."

Gen. Tayler enters the combo mess and sees Lt. Gareth and four soldiers and three very shabby looking people. One appeared to be an old man and the other two appeared to be teenagers, a girl, and a boy.

Gen. Tayler: "Lt Gareth why do your men have bayonets on their rifles."

Lt Gareth: "Sir, these people do not know what a rifle is, but they know what a knife is."

Gen. Tayler: "You are joking."

Lt Gareth: "No sir, they would not cooperate until we put the bayonets on."

Gen. Tayler: "Who are they?"

Lt Gareth: "Sir, they do not speak our language."

Gen. Tayler on his radio; "Gen. Tayler to Gwen Grey,"

Grey, "Yes go ahead."

Gen. Tayler: "Do you have any linguistic experts?"

Grey, "Yes, I do."

Gen. Tayler, "this is important, have them come to the combo mess."

Gwen Grey oversaw the English end of project Camel-Otter. Some said she had the job because her father was senator Veer. But they also said, there would be no project Camel-Otter if it was not for her father. Because of the project, this was not a regular Army base, there was over 120 scientists. They had their on quarters, their own break and exercise room, and from 6 P.M. TO 11:55 P.M. they had their on-club bar, with music and T.V. sets. This was because everyone on the base was a volunteer and had signed a contract. In that contract unless it was a matter of life and death, they could not leave the base. Because it was a scientific base there were 420 individual quarters. For scientist and military alike individual quarters 9 feet by 18 feet. With a single bunk a shower commode and basin.

Now three of her scientists were coming into the mess hall. Tayler knew them, they were Mazak, Timms and Smith. After greeting them Tayler said, "see if you can talk to these people." All three went to the locals and Tayler began to hear jabber. Now smith came to Gen Tayler and said, "they speak incredibly old Germanic."

Gen. Tayler: "You mean they are Germans?"

Smith: "No sir, what I am saying is they are speaking ancient Anglo Saxon, which was Germanic. I believe they are speaking incredibly old English." "Well," Tayler said, "we must detain them." You three oversee them, you have full authority strip them bathe them put Army clothes on them feed them and for tonight put them in the brig.

4

A meeting at Fort Sherwood

An hour later Tayler put the word out for all of Grey's people who were available to come to the conference room. Now there were 80 people in the room with Tayler and Gwen Grey up front. A lot of talk going on, and Gwen Grey got their attention and asked has anyone figured out where we are. Again, there was a buzz and now two scientists stood up and one said, "I think a better question is when we are." Another scientist stood up and said, "I been looking at the stars and star charts and I would say 750 A.D. 50 years either way."

After another loud session, a different scientist stood up and said, "I went up on the radio mast with my telescope and some pictures I had of our surroundings and I would say we are exactly where we were, but at a different time." Tayler looked the room full of scientist over and said, "I would like for everyone who believe we have moved back in time to raise their hand." They nearly all raised a hand. Sam noticed that Dr. Phitto was one of the few that did not.

Gen. Tayler, "Dr. Phitto you do not think we have moved to the past?"

Dr. Phitto; "Time travel is impossible; it would break all the scientific laws." Now there was a lot of noise in the room, some openly criticized Phitto.

Gen. Tayler: "If you do not believe it is possible why are you here?"

Dr. Phitto; "I was on another project, when it ended, they sent me here." As the meeting broke up Tayler saw Phitto was having a deep conversation with Dr. Stenger.

The meeting broke up and Gen Tayler urge them to get together and form a consensus. One of the science technicians stayed behind. "Gen. Tayler, I need to talk to you."

Gen. Tayler; "Go ahead Laszlo." Laszlo went and closed the door.

Laszlo: "Gen Tayler I work on the consoles, and this may have been caused by the fires."

Gen. Tayler; "This what, Laszlo?"

Laszlo: "Sir when the fire was put out the controls on Phitto's console were not set on .1 percent."

Gen. Tayler: "What were they set on?"

Laszlo: "They appeared to be set on 100+ percent."

Gen. Tayler: "Can you prove that?"

Laszlo; "No sir."

Gen. Tayler: "We have video in there."

Laszlo: "Right now, it is not working."

Gen. Tayler: "Well, Laszlo this is dam serious, go get the electrician Valdez, and tell him he is to help you get that video working." "And Laszlo I am to be the first one to see it, no one else." Now Tayler was thinking to himself. This is terrible, one or more traitors in our midst. They may have killed us all. Now I must go to Gwen, he is one of her people.

5

Murder at Fort Sherwood

Gwen, "you are sure about this?"

Gen. Tayler: "Right now, no, Laszlo said right after the fire he found them set at 100+ percent and later found them set where they should have been."

Gwen Gray: "So, you do not have any proof."

Gen. Tayler: "Not till we get these videos working."

Gwen: "All right you have 24 hours then I go public."

Gen. Tayler left Gwen and went to the combo mess hall. He was lucky both Lt. Hall and Master Sargent Johnson were there. Tayler got them off to one side and ask, "have you done an inventory?"

Master Sergeant Johnson: "It has a few estimates in it but yes."

Gen. Tayler: "How long can we feed everybody?"

Johnson; "Regular meals 30 days, lean meals 40 to 45."

Valdez to Tayler, "Gen Tayler come to the control room now."

Gen. Tayler jumped; "Valdez was a serious man he would not be hollering if it were not something big." On the way Tayler thought it might be on fire again. But there was no smoke, Valdez was guarding the door, barely able to speak, his face and eyes red. He let Tayler enter, Tayler was shocked, a man he had talked to 2 hours ago lay dead in a pool of blood.

Lt. Valdez stumbling said, "I went to get more cables, and when I came back, he was like this."

Gen. Tayler on his radio; "Gwen Grey, get Colonel Bradley of the m p's and come to the control room." Two radio clicks, that was a yes.

Gen. Tayler went closer he did not want to step in the blood. It was obvious that Laszlo had been stabbed to death. There were three large stab wounds on his back. He was lying face down. Now Gwen is there and soon Bradley and one of his men were there. Gen. Tayler had to give Bradley all the info he had.

Gwen: Rather cryptic said, "so now you have no witness and no proof."

Gen. Tayler: "Yes, the tapes are gone, we have nothing."

Col. Bradley: "No one enters here till we are through."

Gen. Tayler: "When do we call medical?"

Col. Bradley: "We will call them."

Tayler left; he was pissed Laszlo had been a good man. Now Tayler went to see Lt. Gareth. "I want you to take about 10 armed men outside and circle the berm, looking for anything.

Lt. Gareth; Anything?

Tayler: Anything that could cause us problems. You know what I mean, good bad or ugly we must know our situation, and it is almost dark, do it now.

6

Battle at Fort Sherwood

Thirty minutes later.

Lt. Gareth to Gen. Tayler; "We have incoming."

Now Tayler hears gunshots outside the berm, lots of gunshots, and now silence.

Lt. Gareth; "Gareth to Tayler."

Gen. Tayler: "Go ahead, what the heck happened?"

Gareth: "We were attacked by eight mounted men wielding swords."

Gen. Tayler; "And the results?"

Gareth; "Eight dead bad guys and one dead horse."

Gen. Tayler; "Bring everything inside."

Lt. Gareth; "Everything?"

Gen. Tayler: "Leave no trace outside, cover any blood spots with dirt or leaves."

Gen. Tayler; "Tayler to Gwen Grey."

Gwen; "Go ahead Tayler."

Gen. Tayler; "Need your experts on history and everything else outside toward the gate."

Gwen; "What's up?"

Gen. Tayler: "You will see just get them out there between the complex and the gate."

Gen. Tayler: "Tayler to Lance how is your project?"

Lt. Lance; "About one more hour."

Gen. Tayler to Lance; "Great we need power and lights."

Gen. Tayler to Lt. Green.

Lt. Green: "Green go ahead."

Gen. Tayler; "Take some of your armed men to the gate."

Lt. Green: "Will do, what is up?"

Gen. Tayler: "We had some trouble there may be more."

Tayler is nearly to the area where they have brought the horses and bodies and he sees Lt. Gareth take one of his men's m-4 aim it and fire. Now Gareth and two of his men are running. Tayler looks to see where they are going and sees it is the fuel storage tank and fuel is running out onto the ground. Now Tayler is running and out of breath when he reaches the tank. Gareth's man has already turned the valve off and stopped the flow. The scientist Phitto lays dead in the fuel.

Gen. Tayler: "Dam, Lazlo was right he was the traitor."

Gen. Tayler: "Tayler to Gwen, I need you at fuel storage."

Gwen; "Gwen to Tayler be there soon."

Motor pool is across the drive from fuel storage, and Lt. Marvin and his two men came to fuel storage, "How much did we lose?"

Gen. Tayler; "According to the sight gage about 300 gallons. Can your men save any of it?"

Lt. Marvin: "We will save what we can."

Marvin to his men, "get those empty barrels and shovels and put all this fuel dirt into them. We will separate it later."

Soon Gwen Grey was there.

Gen. Tayler pointing to Phitto, "there is your traitor-killer he tried his best to destroy this project. Lt Gareth was correct in stopping him. I want this closed. Phitto is officially Laszlo's killer and Gareth was correct in shooting him. That fuel is as precious as gold right now we cannot replace it and Phitto knew it. He did not know about the reactor he thought he was going to destroy us."

Gen. Tayler: "Gen Tayler to Col. Bradley, you do not have to find the killer now, he was caught trying to dump all our fuel and executed."

Col. Bradley: "Bradley to Tayler, who was it?"

Gen. Tayler: "It was Dr. Phitto, and you can send someone out to get his body."

7

A Prince at Fort Sherwood

There was a big commotion where they were putting the horses and dead men and Tayler and Gwen quickly made their way there.

Gwen: "Gareth what is going on?"

Lt. Gareth: "We were following orders stripping them getting their clothes and weapons and found one of the bodies was alive." Quickly they found him, and he had a bad chest wound but he was alive.

Gwen: "Gareth have your men take him to medical now." Soon the gravely wounded naked man was on a stretcher being carried to medical.

Gen. Tayler: "Gen Tayler to Cap. Andrews, there is a wounded enemy being brought to medical. Put him in restraints like you have been trained to do."

Dr. Cap. Andrews: "Yes, Gen. Tayler, I know my job."

Gen. Tayler. "Dr. Andrews these are not normal times, we have had an explosion, an attack and a killing in the last few hours."

Dr. Andrews, "sorry Gen. I will do my job." Now she sees the troops carrying a nearly naked man in on a stretcher. They put him on the operating table and begin to apply the restraints. The prisoner comes alive and is trying to break loose. More troops rush in and he is restrained. He is shouting, shouting and Grey and her linguist are there. Andrews asked, "what he is saying?"

Gwen Grey, "he is saying, you can kill him if you want, but you have no right to torture a Knight."

Gwen Grey through one of her linguists, Timms, tells him, "We are not going to torture you. We are going to try to heal you, but you are our prisoner." All this time the doctor had been watching him and began to examine the gaping wound. He seemed to be mesmerized by her and only reacted when she put the mask on his face. She had the gas flowing before that and in a few seconds, he went out staring at Andrews. He was in restraints now and Andrews had him out. Now she turned that over to the doctor/anesthesiologist Lt. Ramones, and now she could study the wound. She told the nurses what she needed and quickly went and prepped. She was aware that the wound would have already killed most men and might still kill him. They took x-rays and pictures. She began the operation, and even though the room was cold, several times in the next three hours she sweated. Now she looked across the table and said, "wake him up." Andrews went into the next room for coffee and to unwind. Now she hears him shouting and goes back in.

Timms, who had stayed through the whole thing, said, "he was just ranting for you." The patient calms down some, but Andrews saw tears in his eyes, and he talks. Timms translates, "he wants to know if he died, and you brought him back from hell." "He must have had a bad dream," said Timms.

Andrews, "tell him no he came close, but did not die." They had heard the rumor that he was a prince, and he had been wearing a gold Torc around his neck. So now they were calling him prince. Timms said, "he wants you to stay in the room for a while." Andrews was dog tired but what the hell, you did not operate on a prince every day. She found a chair and had a nurse bring her a blanket.

8

Hot Water at Fort Sherwood

In his office Tayler is talking to Lance and Nimmer. "All right Nimmer tell us the situation."

Capt. Nimmer, "We must have water to cool the reactor. We have two systems, the main and the backup."

Gen. Tayler, "we know that."

Capt. Nimmer, "Well the main system does not work." "We are using the backup which uses the berm lake. It works but the berm lake is going to get hot and then it will not work."

Lt. Lance, "the berm lake was created as an afterthought, they used the dirt to make the berm and soil is deep here."

Tayler, "I think I know what is wrong, outside the berm all the way around the base there is a dividing line between present and past."

Lance, "so you think the pipes go so far and stop."

Tayler, "Yes, I do."

Nimmer, "how do we repair it?"

Tayler, "well we do not have those large pipes, and I feel we are about 150 feet short. However, I think we could dig a canal."

Nimmer, "can we do it soon, berm lake is going to get hot?"

Tayler to Lance, "you want to handle this?"

Lance, "Yes, I do." Now in the early morning mist, Lance, Nimmer, Sargent Mills, and Lt. Philon are wading through the grass in the area where they think the pipes are and soon both metal detectors are buzzing and then they stop.

Capt. Nimmer, "Dam about 160 feet."

Lance, "Lt. Philon do you have someone that can operate the dozier?"

Philon, "Yes, I do, I will get him on it."

Lt. Lance, "Sargent Mills I want you to have a full squad of armed men here at all times while we are digging this canal." "Locate Col. Murphy and have him send two squads of men out here with picks and shovels. The dozier cannot do it all." Now Lt. lance got his radio out and called Lt. Hobbs the quartermaster, "do we have any cement?"

Lt. Hobbs, "Sir I will have to check."

Philon to Lance, "Sir there is an area on the other side of the river that appear to have a lot of stones."

Lance, "Yes and I have seen a zodiac in the motor pool." Three days later they had two rock lined canals for their reactor. One upstream for cool water and one downstream to dump their water. Berm lake had only been half full so now they were pumping their hot water into it until it was filled.

Gen. Tayler went to the base hospital and found the prince had settle down. He was not in chains now, but he was wearing a dog collar and had to be shocked 4 times before he learned. He was wearing army clothes and looked normal.

Capt. Andrews, "Tayler he is amazing, he learns amazingly fast. He is learning a lot of English. As you can see, he has discovered our shampoo and razors."

Tayler asked, "how are his wounds?"

Andrews, "particularly good, he is healing fast."

Tayler, "when can he travel?"

Andrews, "In a limo now, on a horse, a couple of days."

Tayler, "Is Timms working with him?"

Andrews, Hours every day.

Tayler left the hospital, he had to go see Gwen Grey, she had buzzed him and said they needed to talk.

After good mornings Gwen Grey got right to the point. "A few of my scientist have protested the way you handled Phitto's death."

They want Gareth arrested and charged with murder.

Tayler was infuriated, He said, "I am the supreme commander of this little fort. While we are isolated, I am responsible for keeping us alive. I am judge and jury. They have two choices, stay with my rules or walk out that gate and not come back."

Gwen, "you are joking."

Gen. Tayler, "I am dead serious, Gwen you are my friend but if you and all your scientist want to walk away you can."

9

A Pistol at Cambridge

At Cambridge Senator Veer was waiting in the fancy project office, and he did not like to wait. Now the project manager enters the office. Without hesitation Veer shouts, "dam you Planck where is my daughter?"

Planck, "we do not know."

Veer, "dam its Planck that is not good enough. You told me when you were begging for millions for this project that my daughter would be completely safe."

Planck, "some of our scientist have theories but no proof."

Veer, "what do they think?"

Planck, "they think the whole base was sent to the past."

Veer even more angry, reaches into his coat pocket and pulls out a compact Glock and pointing it at Planck's face said, "you mean your scientist were so screwed up that instead of sending a small object across the ocean, they sent a whole fort into the past." Waving the gun Veer said, "you better find a way to get her back."

10

Taking Prince to Wexford

At Fort Sherwood five days later, they are taking prince home.

Gen. Tayler was leaving Lance in charge with Gwen Grey. "While I am gone you out rank her and here is a paper to prove it." Tayler was taking Andrews, Timms, Gareth, Sgt Mills and six soldiers. They all had some local looking apparel, but they did not look like locals.

They all carried captured swords that Gareth and his men had collected, but they were just for show. About five miles from base they were attacked by approx. 18 men either with lances, bows or drawn swords. Arrows started coming close to them and Tayler did not hesitate; "Mills have your men shoot the three in front." "Is that a direct order sir?" "Yes, it is." There was a huge roar of their weapons and three of the attackers were dead and the others had ridden away. The prince had been shocked and rode away but now rode back to them. Tayler and his people did not stop, they continue on their way. Late that afternoon they arrived at the large but crudely built castle. The first thing they had seen was crudely made small houses with thatch roofs. Next, they came to a wooden stockade type wall made with vertical heavy poles. They went through the gate and were stopped in the courtyard. In front of them was a well-built but barnlike structure, with a wood shingle roof. They were stopped at the entrance and told they would have to leave their weapons outside. Gen. Tayler said no in a very crude way and told Timms to say it that way. Soon Prince and Capt. Andrews went inside. About an hour later they returned with the Kings man who was all smiles. Their horses were taken to the stables and Tayler and his group were led into the large hall with four firepits and an awfully long table with benches for about 30 along the sides and a rough chair at each end. Along the walls of the building were platforms about four feet wide and about one foot high. That was all that was in the hall. Later that night they would find out that nearly all the castles residents would wind up in their bedding on the hall platforms at bedtime. No wonder Prince Zorn thought the brig where he stayed at night was fancy. He had been awed by the flushing toilet.

Now the King and his party entered and after they were seated Gen. Tayler, and his party were seated. Now more people came in and grabbed the few remaining bench seats and several had to sit on the platforms. Tayler had been informed that they would talk after dinner. Dinner it seemed was a roasted half of a cow. Well-cooked and salted but no spices with a few bland vegetables. Soon a barrel of ale was brought in, and everyone was drinking ale. After dinner Tayler, Andrews and Timms were taken into another building like the first but much smaller.it seemed this was the king's home. Now Tayler, Andrews, and Timms with Prince the King and two of his advisors began to bargain. They had a lot to bargain about and there were some language problems. The first thing was basically a peace treaty. Then they went on to other things like hay and cattle and hogs for food. Now it was over, and Prince Zorn led them back into the large hall. Prince proudly showed them platform space he had reserve for them. When Tayler had Timms ask Prince about a facility prince led him to a small privy outside the castle. It had a stone bench with 3 round holes in it. The next morning Prince Zorn was there and at the long table milk, butter, honey and rough bread had been set out. They made the best of it because they wanted to be on their way.

Soon they were saddling their horses and these saddles did not help you much. They did not have stirrups. Tayler decided he would have to find someone who could make real saddles. Tayler had Timms ask Prince Zorn if they had leather for sale. The prince led them to a place outside the stockade among the cottages where there was a stack of not to well processed cow hides. Soon they had made a deal. When Prince started bringing the food and hay, they would bring cow hides too. Now they were on their way. It was not a road it was a trail and when you came to a stream your horse waded it. When they were about halfway back to the base, they were climbing a hill. When they reached the top, they stopped for a few moments to let the horses rest.

11

Trouble in the past

Gareth to Tayler, "we have trouble, there is a war party like yesterday riding this way."

Tayler, "Yes, I see them, do you think they are coming for us?"

Lt. Gareth, "Yes, I do, I think it was their people we killed yesterday."

Gen. Tayler pulled out his cell phone (the base has its own cell tower)

Gen. Tayler to Marvin, "I need you."

Marvin, "what can I do?"

Tayler, "Is the bird fueled and armed?"

Marvin, "Yes sir."

Tayler, "Well get it in the air, head west approx. 5 miles you will see a crowd. They mean to do us harm, we killed some of their people yesterday. Make one pass fast right over their heads Then come and land behind our hill."

Lt. Marvin, "Sir, you are authorizing me and my gunner Sgt. Sanders to use deadly force."

Tayler, "No I want you to scare them." The attacking party is coming up the long slope and their archers are beginning to shoot arrows. In about ten minutes they see a speck in the sky, and it becomes the black chopper with the fake red wings. Marvin does a maneuver to sort things out and then flies away. Some ask why is he leaving?

Tayler, "He is not leaving, he is getting ready." Now they see the chopper flying toward the enemy, as it reaches them his gunner pumps fuel into the turbines exhaust and makes a plume of fire and

25

smoke. Mayhem is happening among the enemy. Marvin flies toward Tayler now.

Tayler, "Land behind the hill so they cannot see you."

Marvin, "Yes sir."

Gen. Tayler and Gareth are looking at the scene through binoculars. They can see people in this group pointing at them and hollering and screaming at each other. Now two people are riding toward them. Lt. Gareth to Sgt. Mills, "have your men put bayonets on their weapons."

Sgt. Mills, "Sir, why?"

Lt. Gareth, "these people do not recognize rifles, they recognize knives." The squad fixed bayonets as the two riders came closer. Now they stopped about 100 feet away.

Tayler told Timms to tell them to come closer. Timms did and now they are about 20 feet away.

Tayler, "why were you going to attack us?"

Older negotiator, "you killed some of our people yesterday."

Timms told Tayler what they said, and Tayler told Timms to tell them they attacked us. There was some talk between the older and younger negotiators. Tayler saw a wild boar at the edge of some trees about 300 feet away.

Tayler, "Sgt. Mills who is your best shot?"

Sgt. Mills, "that would be corporal Brown sir."

Tayler, "well corporal Brown take out that hog over there." A minute later, two shots rang out and the hog flopped over dead. Older and Younger were both startled and impressed.

Now older said, "we will allow you to proceed."

Gen. Tayler, "we do not believe you. We want you and your army to go back to your on lands."

Now younger, "and if we do not?"

Tayler, "we will call the Dragon back."

Now younger says, "you do not control the dragon."

Tayler, "Marvin, lift off just enough for our guest to see you they do not believe you are our friend."

Now from the direction of the chopper comes loud music, and Tayler had to laugh, hell it was The Flight of the Valkyries, and now the chopper arose and came toward them then backed away and out of sight and the music stopped. Both the frightened negotiators said, "we will withdraw" and rode back to their group.

Tayler tells his people his plan. They would wait till they were sure this group had really left then have Marvin confirm it before they left this good position.

Sgt Mills spoke up and said, "there is no reason to let that hog go to waste." Tayler laughed and said, "all right go and butcher it."

About an hour and a half later the helicopter rose from its sheltered position and zoomed ahead of them.

Lt. Marvin called Tayler and said, "it is all right. They are south of our base, still headed east towards their castle."

Tayler, "All right Marvin return to base." Two hours later Tayler and his group were entering their base, happy to be there. Tayler went straight to his office and was surprised that both Lance and Gwen Grey came to meet him.

12

Revolt at Fort Sherwood

Lance, "we have a problem." Grey, "the device scientist say that the way you are operating, you are destroying our world. That if we got back our wives, our children, and our friends would not be there."

Gen. Tayler, Surprised, red faced angry, said, "I know what they are saying, and I would like to comply, but I am responsible for everyone on the base at this time, not that time. What are they going to do shoot me?"

Gwen Grey, "they are not going to work on the device until you start acting more responsible."

Gen. Tayler, truly angry, said, "their little college protest is endangering everyone on this base. We do not know how stable this jump is, it could move us again and scramble us. I understand what they do not like, I do not like it either. But I must do what I do. They can just sit on their asses." Gwen and Lance left, and Tayler went to his footlocker and found his emergency bottle of whiskey, God he needed a drink. Gwen Grey and Lance walked the long hallway of the office building and into the hallway of the quarters building. They came to Gwen Greys quarters and looked in both directions, and quickly both entered. Now they clung to each other, and Lance said, "I hate this." Gwen said, "no more than I do." Now there was several kisses, and now Lance starts for the door.

Gwen, "do not go yet." --

Gen. Tayler tossed and turned all night getting truly little sleep. He went to the combo mess hall and Lance and several others were already there. Tayler had just sat down when cookie sends him a plate of ham and eggs. Tayler tries it and speaking to Lance says, "the hams flavor is good, but it is a little tuff."

Lance, "then you should have your people shoot a tender hog."

Everyone laughed and now Tayler knew he was eating ham from the wild hog, and he laughed too.

13

Two Weeks Later at Washington

Senator Veer was in his office in the senate building. In front of him were two senators of the other party. They were wanting to cut funding to the Camel Otter project.

Sen. Keith, "Senator you keep pouring money into your pet project and we see no results. Remember there is an election coming up." Now they stormed out.

Veer sat there thinking gentlemen I wish I had never heard of the project. Then I would still have my daughter.

14

Melted at Fort Sherwood

Gen. Tayler had decided to just let the scientist situation ride. Tayler saw his job as keeping everybody alive and well.

Col. Bradley to Gen. Tayler, "Come to the main parking lot now. This is important." Tayler jumped up and several others did too, and they ran to parking lot. When they got there, they found Bradley standing about 50 feet from a smoldering mess about the size of a car. It was not far from the cars and pick-ups sitting in the parking lot.

Gen. Tayler to Murphy, "what was it?"

Col. Bradley crying, "I was just here by accident, and I saw this thing appear out of thin air. It was trying to become solid. There was a man in it trying to speak to me and it all just sort of melted."

Tayler, you think it was a time machine.

Bradley, "Yes, I think they were trying to contact us."

Tayler saw Gwen Grey had come and went to her and said, "if your scientists are not too busy, they need to come and investigate this."

15

At Cambridge, they are Changing Time.

Senator Veer's phone buzzed, he picked it up and his secretary said, "IT'S Planck." Veer picked up the phone.

Sen. Veer says, "this is Veer."

Planck, "Senator we have troubles."

Sen Veer, "I know, my daughter is missing."

Planck, "yes sir, but there is a lot more that I cannot tell you on the phone. Can you come to the project?"

Sen. Veer, "Dammit Planck I do not want to."

Planck, "there are some top-secret things I need to tell you."

Sen. Veer, "All right Planck, in about three hours. I am not happy."

Planck, "I will be expecting you."

Three hours later Veer walks from the limo into the project.

Sen. Veer, "Planck you son of a bitch start talking."

Planck, "we built a device large enough to carry a man and sent it back. It could not stabilize and melted down killing the man in it."

Sen. Veer, "that is terrible, but you brought me down here to tell me that?"

Planck, "No, what is way more important is they are changing time."

Sen. Veer, "they are doing what?"

Planck, "before we started this project, we recorded a billion records in a devise, in a devise that is untouchable. And now a lot of those records do not match public records. Births, deaths and events are changing."

Sen. Veer, "why is that happening."

Planck, "well if someone dies that did not die in the normal timeline their descendants would disappear from history if it were one or one hundred."

Sen. Veer, "so you say our base is changing history."

Planck, "You or I could disappear tomorrow."

Sen. Veer, "you mean die."

Planck, "No does not die I mean never existed."

Sen. Veer, "God Planck what can we do?"

Planck, "we only have two options, build a device that can bring the base back. Or we send a large bomb to the middle of the base."

Sen. Veer, "Are you crazy!"

Planck, "No Veer you can talk to any scientist about timeline, and they will tell you how serious it would be."

Sen. Veer, "you are saying I might have to authorize killing my own daughter."

Planck, "it might come to the bomb or 10 million people dying." Senator we have open this thing up. There are three huge companies with top security clearance that wanted in on this and we have given them everything we have. They realize the danger and will work on the device. If any of the three can bring the base back safely they will receive five billion dollars. That was secretly authorized by the president, a group of scientists showed him how serious this is.

Sen. Veer, "God what a mess, I will be staying at the Mark Plaza hotel here in the city and I will be here for news every day." Now in the limo Veer surprises the driver who has worked for him many years. We are going to my residence so I can pack a bag. Then we come back to the Mark Plaza hotel, and I will get you a room too. We will be staying there for a while.

16

Delivery at Fort Sherwood

Tayler left the grisly scene and Lance went with him. Their first stop was the motor pool which besides the chopper had a dozier, a hum v, a jeep ambulance, a small fork truck, a field kitchen trailer and two civilian motorcycles. Lt. Marvin told them they had saved about 50 gallons of the spilt fuel. Next, they went to the garden spot that was being cleared and cultivated by volunteers. It was shaping up. Now Lt. Francis at what once was the base riding club.

Lt. Francis, "Sir we are out of hay and the grass is going fast because we have so many more horses."

Gen. Tayler, "we have purchased hay from the west castle." Tayler's phone buzz and he answered, it was the main gate.

Lt. Jones, Sir, "we have visitors."

Gen. Tayler, "how many?"

Sir, it is the Prince and several carts.

Tayler, "I will be right there." When he got there of course Prince Zorn wanted to see Andrews, but Tayler said, "help me first." There were four carts of hay that he sent to Lt. Francis, then there were the hides that he sent to Lt. Brown, a cart of vegetables went to the mess. Now Tayler and Johnson discuss the two hogs. They had no place or food for them.

Tayler says, "take them out of hearing and slaughter them." And then there were two scrawny milk cows that he sent to Lt. Francis. Once that was done Tayler took Prince up to the combo mess hall and called Andrews to come to the mess hall. Andrews came and Tayler could tell they were very happy to see each other. Tayler went on his way and started contacting people to see if they had got their shipments.

Lance had Johnson cook a large meal for Prince and everybody and it was a happy occasion. Then Lance, Andrews, Grey and Tayler took Prince to the scientist club where he was fascinated of the video of a pro football game. Later Prince was totally happy to sleep in the brig.

The next morning Lance was watching Prince gather up his people, they had all camped out by Lt. Francis stable. Sarg. Johnson had sent food to them. Now they were hitching up their crude oxen puled carts. Prince wanted to see Andrews again, so Lance took him to the mess hall. Lance did not let it show that he found Prince joy in using forks and spoons amusing. Now lance and Tayler were watching Prince and three armed men on horses and the rest on the two wheeled ox carts as they left Fort Sherwood.

The Fort Sherwood Scientist

Later Tayler, Lance, Nimmer, Grey and Col. Bradley got together to talk about the scientist situation. It seemed that after seeing the tragedy in the parking lot they had changed some.

Col. Bradley, "my people say it is two scientist that were buddies of Phitto, one named Stenger are the ones who are the leaders of the protest."

Tayler, "do not they understand that if they worked hard, they might repair the device and take us back." Now Tayler put out word for all scientist to come to the mess hall. They gathered and for twenty minutes there was a lot of bitching. Then Tayler gets up to talk.

Tayler, "A lot of you do not like me, and a lot of you do not like the way I am running things. You say I am damaging our timeline, well people yes, I am. What you do not seem to realize is this base just

35

sitting here effects our timeline. To save our timeline we must take the base back to our time. The longer it sits here the more effect it will have on the more locals I will have to deal with. So, if you are serious about saving our timeline you will get into the lab and work your butts off to fix the device." There was some loud discussion but basically, they seemed receptive, and the meeting was over.

People at Fort Sherwood's gate

Two days later Gen. Tayler's radio buzz, Lt. Jones, "sir we have people at the gate."

Tayler, "how many?"

Lt. Jones, "Six sir."

Tayler replied that he was on the way. Now he buzzes Timms and told him to go to the gate. When Tayler got to the gate, he was a little surprised that two of the six were the two negotiators. Two were very fierce looking warriors that looked angry and two were dressed better and had a little gold showing. Tayler guessed that they might be princes or something. The older introduced himself, he was John River, next he introduced Prince Silas of the red hair, and Prince Paul who can read. Timms translated what John read off a parchment. Our king is an old and wise man, he has talked to many people about what has happened between us. And the king asked do you want peace?

Tayler, "yes, we do."

Timms translating John says, they suggest a hostage swap which is common among these people.

Tayler, "we want peace, who do they offer?"

Timms, "The two prince's sir."

Tayler "wow he was surprised." Tayler turned to Lance, "set up a good, large tent put good cots and blankets in it. Put a large table and chairs in it, these talks may take a while."

Lance, "you mean bring them inside."

Tayler, "Yes, I do, set it up on the parking lot, but keep a couple of guards watching them but they cannot feel like they are prisoners."

Lt. Hall and two dozen soldiers did what they had done many times before and in 90 minutes a real army campsite was set up. Soon Lt. Johnson's people had brought them food and water. To say that the visitors were awed would be putting it mildly.

Tayler, Grey, Lance and several scientists were having a meeting in the mess hall.

Grey, "do you think they are serious?"

Tayler, "Yes, I do. They have learned what our weapons can do."

Their older wiser ones know numbers do not matter much when the enemy has better weapons.

Lance, "all right, who do we send." They have asked for someone.

Of importance. And strangely they have asked for a corporal Brown and her weapon to be the king's bodyguard while she is there.

Grey, "what is that about?"

Tayler laughed, "she killed a wild hog with her M-4 at over 100 yards and impressed them." Taylor buzz Sgt. Mills, "will you send. Corporal Brown to the mess hall. No, it is not for K.P. duty."

Grey, "well it cannot be us three, who do we send."

Col. Bradley, who was in the discussion spoke up and said, "I am one of the next ranks and I will go." There was discussion around the table and then all agreed yes. Now brown arrives and they explain the offer.

Corp. Brown, "I never met a king before yes, I will go."

Now the top three went back to the tent and the big table.

They tell the East reps. Yes, Brown will go and tell them we suggest Col. Bradley.

John River, "This Bradley he is the head of your guards?"

Grey, "Yes, but more than that he is our number four person."

River and Younger and the two princes left the table and huddled. After a short while they came back and asked an unusual question, "would he take his weapon and would he serve as a king's guard."

Tayler stood up and asked John, "will you walk with me." John said, "yes" and they left the tent. Timms walked with them to translate.

Tayler "why are you asking for armed guards." John hesitated.

Then John River said "lately there has been turmoil in our kingdom, there has been one open revolt, and one attempt on the king."

Tayler, "answer me truthfully, is he a bad king."

John, "no he is a good king, but some of the knights want to go to war, claim more land and pillage. That was some of them that first attacked you and came back and lied about you."

Tayler, "all right we agree to the terms of the swap we will talk about other things tomorrow." Now Tayler collected his people, and they went to the mess. Tayler told Sarg. Johnson to send food to them now and later from his club stores send them some wine and beer. Now at a mess table Grey, Tayler, Lance and Bradley discuss the swap. We will send a gun safe with you and any time you or Brown are not in control your weapon it must be locked up. How much ammo should they take? Probably about three or four clips each. How about the new Kevlar version of our uniforms? How about one set of night vision? How about a few rolls of toilet paper and they all laughed? Now it broke up they each had other things they had to do. The next morning Lance and Grey went to the Windmere people's campsite and invited them to the mess hall. They accepted and were soon enjoying breakfast. Tayler and Lance wanted to impress them, and it seemed to be working. Tayler called LT. Marvin and told him to make sure the motor pool was locked up tight. Then he called Sgt. Mills and ask if he had a portable 50 and Mills said yes, and Tayler asked him to set it up using the berm as a backstop and impress our visitors. Even the two fierce visiting warriors were shocked by it. Tayler, Lance and Grey and River and Younger worked out a peace treaty and had it signed by noon. Brown had a large backpack, a war vest and carried her M-4, Bradley had a large backpack a bullet proof vests a holster on an ammo belt and his Glock in the holster. They were taking base horses so they would have them when they needed them. They had decided at the last minute that Timms had to go with them at least for a while and now they all rode away.

17

Going to Windmere

As they rode along Brown felt strange, she did not know why she had accepted this job. It was probably pride in her shooting. They had been riding nearly four hours and were starting up another hill and there it was on the top of the hill. Windmere, they called it and it had a moat and a small brook ran down the hill out of the moat. It had been built on a spring. The gate was already open and as they rode through the gate Brown saw the hinges looked rusty. When Bradley had Timms ask about quarters, he was basically told to put his stuff on a side platform. When that would not work, they were introduced to the armorer, Traxler who had a separate building for making and storing armor and weapons. He looked at their weapons greedily, but Timms let him know they were off limits. They were informed that only royalty had privacy, and they had their on small separate building. There was the great hall, the king's hall, the armory, the larder and the kitchen. The King his brother and their wives and children all lived in the king's hall. At dinner they were instructed to sit at the middle of the long table with their weapons. They saw the royals but were not introduced to them. They slowly got to be around the king, and it was only at certain times. Most of those times there were people in the castle the king did not trust. One day Brown and Timms were walking around, they had watched both the blacksmith and the armorer work in their different shops and had quickly walked past where they butchered the animals. And they were joined by a young man, and he began to talk to Brown through Timms. You do not like the butcher place? Brown, no it is awful. Richard, I do not like it either. They walked around the castle for a long time, and it was only later that she found out who Richard was. The next afternoon Brown had got the utensils out of her mess kit and was using them at this evening meal. She felt she was being watched and looked up. It was Richard watching her eat and she was embarrassed and finished quickly and left. She went to the Armory; it was about the only private place she had. Traxler would be in the hall until it went quiet. Suddenly she was surprised someone was in the darkened room. She heard them talking but did not know what they were saying. Now she hears Timms say, do not be afraid the king's son is trying to apologize. Brown tell him he has nothing to apologize for. Timms and Richard talk and Timms says he asked if he could see you tomorrow and you show him those dinning tools. Brown tells Timms tell him yes that would be all right. Silently Richard was gone. Brown found her bedroll in the dark. She had an army flashlight, but its batteries would not last forever, like the batteries in her night vision scope. Brown thought about this place a fireplace, an open fire, a torch, a candle and an oil lamp were their sources of manmade light. Her M-4 was in the gun safe, but unknown to anyone was always a Glock 43 inside her uniform. She was sure Bradley had a derringer in his boot. Sometimes Bradley or Timms snored but their presence was a comfort.

Tayler and Lance had put the two princes in a room in the scientist quarters. It had two army bunks an army dresser a small shower and a commode, they were amazed. The mess hall was explained to them. Lance took a long time explaining there was a lot of places on the base they could not go. They were entranced by electricity and lights. Two nights later they discover the scientist club, and a woman scientist was drinking a strawberry daiquiri and the red drink taste so good they had to have a second one and they were not used to alcohol.

Tayler had word that some scientist was coming to see him, and he did not know what to expect. Tom Chang was their leader, and he began; we have been watching you and we see your ways have improved. And yes, we realize the best thing to do is fix the device and jump out of here. So, we will be working as fast as we can. Tayler really wanted to choke them, but he hid it. He ate his pride for everyone's sake and thanked them and said he would try to please them in the future. Now they left and again Tayler went to his footlocker.

18

An invite to Wexford

Prince Zorn came to Fort Sherwood to invite some of the people to his kingdom's annual games of course the first person he sought out to invite was Capt. Andrews, he hugged her and said I have to have another name, then he kissed her and pulling away she smile and said you may call me Sarah. Zorn grin showing his white teeth and said a beautiful name. Zorn said my people are having their annual games the next two days. We want you and some of your friends to come. How Sarah asked. Zorn answered, we would leave before daylight and be there by midmorning. "Yes," Sarah Andrews said "I will go." And now Andrews let Zorn kiss her without pulling away. Zorn now says, "let us go see Lance." They went to his office and Grey was there and Zorn invited them both. They both accepted and after some conversation Zorn said "we must go and invite Tayler." They went to Tayler's office and invited him. He thanked them for the invitation, but somebody must stay to run this place. After they left Tayler's office Zorn said, "can we go to that place you call a club?" "Yes," Sarah Andrews said, "and we will invite Gwen and Lance." The four talked, laughed, drank and ate tidbits prepared by Sargent Johnson's staff. Until 10 o'clock and Gwen and Lance left. Zorn and Sarah stayed until 11 and when Zorn kissed Sarah goodnight at her door, she kissed his ear and whispered, "you do not sleep in the brig tonight." The four were on their way before daylight because there was a full moon and Zorn was totally familiar with the terrain. They were at Wexford by midmorning, and the games had already started. They took their horses and packs to the royal stable,

43

and now ventured out into the crowd. There were a lot of people there, many from other kingdoms. A man was selling ale from a large barrel, in an oxcart Food was being sold. They walked past two men turning a spit with a whole beef carcass roasting, its legs anchored to its belly. The contest going on now was the stone toss. A man would toss a ten-pound stone as far as he could and not step out of the circle. Over there was an exceptionally large kettle with two women cooking something that did not smell good. The stone toss finished, and they started the pole toss. A man would try to toss a piece of wood as large as a man's thigh and eight feet long. Now they were having their first horse race, there would be several. Their saddles were not particularly good, and they did not have stirrups. Because of that a man fell off and got stepped on by another horse. Lance mentioned it to Zorn, and he laughed and said it happens all the time. Lance thought to himself, yes because you got bad saddles. Now the Sherwood visitors went to the barnlike castle for a midday meal. The barn like structure had four fire pits but they were only used for heating, food was prepared in a structure next door. Some contests were going on even at mid-day, like knife and ax throwing with people betting on them. The four went back out and they were having the first archery contest, this one for short bows only. Some of them were quite good. Next, they were having another horse race, a long one. Lance saw people making bets and this was a four-lap race. The race was over now and one of the horses had fell and died. Two bad looking men from another kingdom began attacking two others and Lance and Zorn jumped in to stop the trouble. The two that started it looked at them with hate. They walked back by where the beef was roasted and saw nearly all of it had been sold. The long bow archery contests were starting, and Zorn bought them ale. Zorn and Andrews disappear for an hour. The archery contests were still on when they returned. At sundown they went into the castle. The king was giving a feast that night. They saw that all the king's staff were busy mainly preparing food. At dark they were called to dinner and there was an abundance of food. Lance looked at the table and saw beef, pork and birds. The king gave a short talk and then everyone went for the food, soon people were tossing scraps and bones to the palace dogs. The dogs did what they were supposed to do and kept the floor clean. After the meal three different troubadours sang songs that the Fort Sherwood people did not understand. The torches were put out and that told everyone it was over. Lance, Andrews and Gwen found places on one of the sleeping platforms along the side of the castle and open their bedrolls. Lance whispers I think we should leave at mid-day tomorrow and they agreed. The next morning there was plenty of food, but it was considerably basic, milk, butter, honey and rough bread. The Sherwood people partook of it and then went out to the contest after some small events they started what Zorn called one of their main events. It was the blunt sword contests. It was a long series of two men fighting each other equipped with just a shield and a sword with no point and no sharp edge. However, as they watched a long series of these fights, they saw several bad wounds. Now they were telling Zorn goodbye, and he took them to the palace stable to get their horses. They rode out of Wexford and Zorn rode with them about two miles. Zorn and Andrews did several hugs and kisses before he turned back. It was sundown when they rode into Fort Sherwood, and they quickly went to their normal jobs.

19

Trouble from Wexford

Two days later, Gareth to Tayler, "we got a problem outside the gate."

Tayler, "I will be right there, what is it?"

Gareth, "over 100 people I think they are from Wexford," "yes, I believe they are from Wexford." Tayler got to the gate and went outside. People were crying obviously very distraught. Now two of them that Tayler recognized from the negotiations came to him.

Trandahl spoke quickly, "the prince and the king are near death from wounds, Andrews must save them she must, and Trandahl broke down weeping." Tayler saw he was in terrible grief.

Tayler pulled out his radio, "Tayler to Andrews need you at the gate, gravely injured patient."

Andrews, "I am on my way."

Tayler to Marvin, "Tayler to Marvin, bring the jeep ambulance to the gate now, emergency."

Marvin, "yes sir we are on our way."

Tayler went to the two carts and saw both men were bandaged but there was blood everywhere. He wanted to ask what happened but that would come later. He looked up and saw Andrews running with her bag and Lance and Doctor Ramones right behind her. And looking toward the motor pool Tayler saw the jeep ambulance. Tayler had studied both men and both were gravely wounded, he had to decide. He went to Andrews and said, "you load up the king, take him to the hospital and start working on him, now." Andrews crying said "I must help Zorn. "Tayler stopped her. "This is a direct order. You go take care of the

46

king," Andrews gave in loaded the king in the jeep and they sped away. Doctor Lt. Ramones was working on the prince and Tayler went to her and said, "you will work with him on table two. We do not have time to do one then the other." "I will go now and get as much help as I can."

20

At Cambridge Time quakes

It was the middle of the night and Veer's phone had rung, rang, rang and he had ignored it. Now someone was banging on his hotel door. Veer staggered to it after he heard his driver's voice. Now he opened the door.

The driver said, "Mr. Planck wants you right now." Veer threw on some clothes and took the elevator down to the waiting limo. "What the hell was Planck doing now." It was the middle of the night his driver walked in with him.

Senator Veer says, "all right Planck what is the emergency?"

Planck, "I do not know what they are doing, but whatever it is it is sending shockwaves through the records."

Senator Veer, "what can we do?"

Planck, "Drink coffee and watch."

21

Medics at Fort Sherwood

Tayler over the P. A. system, "all personnel with medic or medical training report to the hospital we need your help," "this is particularly important to our safety and wellbeing." The two regular nurses were there, and Tayler added volunteers to them. Andrews and her team were already striping the king down getting x rays. Then she had to step back and decide what to work on first. They had just brought Zorn in, and Ramones was doing the same thing to him. Andrews thought I cannot let that distract me. She had to type the king's blood and hoped they had a match. She hollered at Tayler "I need blood".

Tayler, Gareth, Mazak an armed squad and two medics went down to the crowd outside the gate. They ask who would like to help the king live. Nearly all said they would, but Tayler narrowed it down to twelve men and five women that would go to the base hospital to be typed and maybe give blood. When they got there, they were amazed by the hospital and two medics demonstrated what they needed to do. Of the twelve there were nine with matching blood, and eight who were willing to give blood. After those eight gave blood, they were given a glass of orange juice and an army blanket to keep. Then the nineth decided he would give too.

Andrews, working on the king, "get that blood hooked up to him tighten those straps.," "I cannot knock him out yet." It was x ray, probe, clean, repair, sew, he had lost so much blood. His blood pressure was much too low. She had three blood bags feeding into him at the same time. It was radical but this was not a normal situation. Clean and sew, all the wounds were blade wounds either slash or stab.

Tayler to Gareth, "Gareth take those volunteers back and get some more, we may need more."

Tayler looked at this operating room, it was large it was very well equipped, it had the latest devices but right now it looked like a slaughterhouse. All the old bloody bandages they had taken off them, new discarded bandages, bloody gloves and instruments. Tayler watched as time went by the doctors working sometimes hollering, more volunteers, more giving blood. Prince Zorn was still losing blood, Ramones was trying to stop it. Working on the king Andrews could hear what Ramones and her crew were saying as they tried to save the prince. She desperately wanted to go to the Zorn, but she had to save the king.

Now lance brought a wounded knight to Tayler, he had a bad cut on his left arm that a medic had worked on.

Lance, this knight can tell us what happened.

The knight began, "as you know it was our people that you had your first clash with." "Seven of our knights killed and our prince Zorn nearly killed." Well some of our people were terribly angry at the king for making peace with you. They thought we should go to war with you. Well some of those knights there for the games joined them in their plan to take over the kingdom. Four of our knights planned to kill the king and take over the kingdom. Four knights from Hedge Dom joined them. The king and prince had five knights with them when they were attacked.

Tayler, "what happened?" "The knight continued, the king, prince and knights fought hard. You see what happened to the king and prince, three of his knights were killed and I was injured. Four of the attackers were killed and two ran away. Two have taken over the kingdom." when it became known how gravely injured the king and prince were, they came back and sit on the throne. They rule the kingdom now.

Andrews finished her work with the king, the nurses were still doing their many things. She felt she could step back for a moment. She looked at prince and the team working on him. Oh god he was hurt so bad. She went into the prep room totally cleaned up and put-on clean scrubs and went back into the king and rechecked everything. Retelling the crew what to do and if you run out of blood tell Tayler to get more. Now she let herself go close to the prince table. She was shaking, she knew why Tayler had ordered her to take care of the king. She had to many emotions involve with the prince. Her involvement with him was so strained.

22

Another Prince at Windmere

Tayler went to Lance and said, "have tents set up for those people like we did the others."

Lance, "Gareth is working on that now."

Tayler looked at the king and said, "if they survive, we must help them get their kingdom back." Lance went down to the throng of people, Gareth and Gwen Grey were there trying to get everything set up.

Gareth, "we are not set up for this. We are setting up eight tents on the main parking lot, but they are four different kinds. We only have one field kitchen trailer and one water trailer."

Lance, "what about latrines?"

Gareth, "One of Marvin's people is bringing five porta potty latrines with the fork truck."

Gwen Grey, "Lance I need to talk to you." Lance goes off to one side with her.

Lance, "all right, what is it?"

Gwen Grey, "these people are talking about another prince, and that they need him." Lance went and found Mazak and questioned him.

Mazak, it seems that Prince has a younger brother who is a hostage at Windmere. And the people are thinking that if Prince and the king die the younger brother would be king. Lance was thinking about all the implications. Lance motioned to Gwen Grey, and they went to Tayler. In Tayler's office they were having a discussion. The consensus was that the young prince was in grave danger. He was in danger from both Windmere and Wexford.

Lance, "we must go get him."

Gwen Grey, "what if Windmere does not want to give him up."

Tayler, "John River said his king was a good wise man, if he is, he will release him."

Lance, "what is the king and prince condition?"

Tayler, "it could go either way, we need to go get that prince now."

Lance, "I will go, I will take two squads with me, all on horses. We should be gone within an hour. Soon he was looking for the troops over, they were under Lt. Gareth well-armed, Helmets and backpacks." Even pushing the horses, it was nearly dark when they reached Windmere. Lance stopped the troops a half mile from Windmere only he and Sgt. Mills rode up to the open gate. Sgt. Mills ask the two guards if they would get John River. The guards did not leave their post but hollered at someone inside the castle. Soon River and Younger appeared. They saw the troops in the distance and demanded to know why they had brought so many armed men. Lance and Mills spent a good while telling them everything that had happened. Now river changed, showing compassion for what had happened. Now river said, you came for the prince for now he may be king.

Lance, yes, we must get one of them back on the throne.

River, come into the castle then, it is dark, plan on staying all night.

Lance pulled out his phone, glad the base cell tower was in range and called Gareth. "Camp there for the night and watch both your front and your back, Wexford might show up."

Gareth, "Yeah, we had thought of that, we have three sets of night vision."

Now river and Younger take Lance and Smith in through the gate and a stable hand takes their horses. They lead them into the large hall. It was mealtime and it looked like they were at least halfway through it. Lance saw dogs were already chewing on mealtime bones that had been tossed to them. River talked to someone and now room was made for them at the table. Lance now saw Brown and Bradley and spoke to them. After the meal there was a period of waiting and they talked to Brown and Bradley and gave them a very brief rundown. Lance had noticed a young man around Brown, and she introduced him as prince Richard. Now they were led into smaller building and the king and his advisors and Rivers and Younger were there. They had to go through the proper ritual of meeting the king and them being introduced to the king. Then Rivers proceeded to tell the king why they were there. Then the king wanted them to tell him in detail everything that had happen at Wexford. It took a while, but Lance and Mills did it. They are asked to step back and the king and his advisors huddle for quite a while. Now they motion for Lance and Mills to come close again. The king asks do usurpers now set on the throne. Yes, Lance said, the king and crown prince are gravely wounded and are at Fort Sherwood. Now the king asked, do you want to take over Wexford? Lance replied, no we want to place the rightful person back on the throne whether it is king or prince. The king now says, the king does not have enough knights to retake the castle. Lance had to answer this carefully, we will help the king regain his kingdom. The king replied, do you plan to take over Wexford?

Lance, we have no desire to take over anyone. The king's chief advisor comes forward then and ask Lance will you vow on your honor that you and your people will restore the proper ruler. Lance says yes. The advisor motions to two knights standing over against a wall to come to him. They do and the advisor tells them what to do. The advisor places them in front of Lance facing him and both draw their swords and hold them pointing upward. An old grey man who Lance had not even noticed before came and stood behind the knights. He held up some sort of symbol and ask Sir Lance do you swear on you and your families honor that you will do everything in your power to place the rightful heir on the Wexford throne? Lance Said yes, I do in English, and then the advisor gave him some strange words to say. Now the knights and the old man went away and the king through Rivers told them, yes, we will release the prince. And now the good-looking young man came to Mills and began asking him about his family.

Soon after talking to Brown and Bradley for a few minutes they were saddling up. Lance felt it best to get the prince surrounded by Fort Sherwood troops. Soon they were in Gareth's camp in bedrolls under the stars with four troops vigilant. They were up at first light and Mills showed the prince how to manage a M R E. Now they were on their way Lance was happy that things had went well but was wary of what might happen. They arrived at Fort Sherwood at noon and the first thing Lance and Mills did was take the prince to see his father and brother. He was shocked at how badly they had been injured, and amazed that they were still alive. The two princes talked animatedly in their language until Andrews broke it up telling Zorn that he had to rest, and Lance noticed that she kissed Zorn on the cheek. The king had survived but was still in such bad shape he was not allowed to talk. Alfred, the younger prince, held his hand and talked to him. Now lance turned Alfred over to Mills to instruct him about the base. Lance went to his quarters to clean up and was surprised by a knock but was not to surprise to find it was Gwen Grey.

Lance pulled her into the room kissed her and was amazed at how fresh and beautiful she always looked. How do you do it, Lance asked? Do what, Grey replied. Very few women who are as smart as you are managed to look like you do and have the aura that you do. Lance, you do not have to B S me you know how much I care for you. Lance, no B S, you think I would be this crazy over a regular woman?

23

We have To Capture Wexford

A short while later Lance was with Tayler. Lance was saying, Tayler we cannot wait for the king to recover. Every day we wait those criminals become more entrenched in power.

Tayler, I know, what do you want to do?

Lance, I want to take a force and take it back.

Gen. Tayler, Details Lt. Lance, tell me details.

Lance, well I would take all the kings' men and about half of our troops. I would surround the castle and with bull horns ask them to surrender. Which they will not do. So, I would start lobbing in teargas which should make a lot of people come out. The bad guys would go up on the roof and ramparts to get away from the gas. They will have archers up there, but we have sharpshooters that can pick the archers off.

Tayler, what about the bad guys that sit on the throne?

Lance, I do not know, I assume they will be on the roof too.

Tayler, do you have someone who is good with a M-79 or a grenade launcher?

Lance, I will have to get with Major Mills, I am sure we have two or three that can use one.

Tayler, all right, I am being the bad guy what if that does not work.

Lance, we could either starve them out or storm it.

24

Chaos in Washington

Washington D. C. A special small group has been created by the president and right now hollering and arguing is going on. The people were handpicked by the president and his advisors, and they have just been told part of the situation.

One elder senator shaking his finger at the president you let this happen.

The president answered, I only found out about this project two weeks ago.

A long-time congressman asked are you going to have them arrested and tried for this.

The president answered I cannot, they have not broken any laws. Another congressman are you crazy, they are destroying our world and they have not broken any laws.

You tell me what laws they broke, the president replied.

Another said there must be laws against time travel.

The president said no one thought it was possible. Then there was more shouting and talking.

25

The Fight for Wexford

Tayler, I do not like the idea of starving them out it might take too long.

Gwen Grey came in then and asked, "starving who out?"

Lance, "we are discussing how we are going to get Wexford back; we do not want to cause a lot of damage to it."

Gwen Grey, "no that would be counterproductive, but how will you get it back?"

Tayler told the planning he and Lance had been doing.

Gwen Grey, "that sounds good, when will this start?"

Tayler, "in two days, I want to know a little more about the king's condition, and we have a lot of planning to do." Tayler pulled out his phone and punch the number for Sgt. Mills. Soon Sgt. Mills was in Gen. Tayler's office and Gwen Grey left.

Lance talking to Mills, "we are going to capture Wexford and we need to plan it." For the next two hours they went over it and now they are with the quarter master Hobbs checking their supplies.

Hobbs, we still have a lot of M.R.E.s even though we have given the Wexford people quite a few.

Tayler, how about ammo?

Hobbs, "we have plenty for the AR-15 and M-4, we do not have a lot for the helicopter gun."

Lance, "do we have grenades for a M-79 or M-203?"

Hobbs, "yes it seems we have a good supply of M-381s."

Lance, "what is that?" Hobbs answered, "regular explosive." Then Lance asks him if there was any tear gas. And Hobbs looked further and said, "yes, we have a good supply of M-651s and look there we have some M-397s."

Tayler, "what kind are they?"

Hobbs, "they are new they are air burst."

Lance, "hey those may come in handy."

The planning was busy and working with Mazak, Smith, Erick and Taggard to get all the Wexford warriors lined out on what they were to do. And this was not to kill their friends and relatives it was to put the king back on the throne and let them go home.

They started before daylight 57 Wexford men most of them on horses, 20 base troops on horses, 80 base troops on foot. Both the hum-vs were loaded with equipment, and both pulled large generators. Tayler was riding in the jeep ambulance, and it was pulling a water trailer. It was early afternoon when they got there and no reaction out of the castle. They surrounded the stockade set up the lights and generators. Lance had already taught the leader of the king's troops to use a bull horn and now he puts him on it. He demands they surrender, and they will be dealt with fairly. Their reply is about a dozen arrows. Tayler goes to Mills and tells him to put 6 gas grenades inside the stockade. Mills picks one of his men that has a M-79 and one that has a M-203 on his M-4 and tells them what to do. Soon the grenades go into the yard surrounding the hall. Within ten minutes the gate is opening, and people are coming out. The king's people take charge of them, but they are just servants and workers. Now Tayler signals Mills for six more gas grenades. Several more people come out, but there is a shower of arrows from guard positions atop of the hall. Two men are hit by arrows and the medics are treating them. Lance gets with Tayler, and they decide to send a different message. Lance goes to Mills and tells him have you men put some bullets where those arrows are coming from. There was a burst of rifle fire an archer screamed and fell out of his nest.

Three more obviously collapsed, a few more arrows and another burst of rifle fire. Lance went to Mills and regretfully told him to put three gas grenades inside the hall and hope it does not catch on fire. They make loud bangs, and they hear some screams and now wounded, warriors come out. Tayler signals Mills to do it again. There are more screams and almost anticlimactic more warriors come out and surrender. The kings chief knight Erick who had used the bull horn pointed at two of those surrendering and said those are the ones we want. Erick and a dozen of his men took possession of those two and Tayler and his people watched the group walk away. Tayler went to some of the king's people and said, "go and search the castle put out any fires." A knight named Taggard asked Lance to come with him into the castle. He wanted to retrieve the treasury. Lance was surprised that the treasury was just a strongbox with maybe a two hundred small gold and silver coins in it. Taggard carried it out to be taken to the king. A short time later Tayler saw Erick and his men coming back but the two traitors were not with them. Lance asks Erick did you let them go? Erick indignant, no we killed them. Tayler to all his people, "pack up load up it is time for us to go." Tayler told Erick and Taggard they were in charge until they brought the king or Zorn back.

26

Sen. Veer sees A Glock in a T.V.

Senator Veer was watching the news when he got the shock of his life. The newsman said a very strange thing has been reported. Archeologist excavating the ancient castle of Windmere found the bones of a young woman. What they cannot explain is how a Glock 43 came to be with the bones. It was a shock; Veer knew his daughter was in that area and he knew she owned a Glock 43. Veer called Planck, "did you see the news about the Windmere castle." "Yes", said Planck.

Veer, "Dam it to hell Planck my daughter is back there, and she owns a forty-three." "Get her out of there before she dies".

27

They had won Wexford

It was getting dark, but Tayler did not care he wanted to get away, and the jeep and hum-vs had headlights. They would space them out to give the troops light. The troops should have been in a good mood, it was a win. Lance did not know why but it did not feel like a win. All Lance wanted to do was get back to the base and get Grey in his arms. He hated that they had to stay secret, but someday this would be over. Going was slow at nighttime with no road, it was midnight when they got back to base. After dismissing the troops Tayler and Lance went to the hospital. Tayler had phoned Andrews when they got back, and she was waiting for them. She told them the king was a lot better and stable now, and Zorn was a lot better. Tayler went to his quarters and Lance debated about going to Veer's, but then thought no I am dirty and smelly, but when he opened his door, someone was there.

Three days later Tayler, Lance and several more were at breakfast in the mess hall when they were surprised by a nurse pushing Zorn in. He was escorted by Andrews and Alfred, there was applause from the troops. They had breakfast together and decided to go to Tayler's office afterward. When they got there for the meeting there was Tayler, Grey, Lance, Zorn, Alfred, and Andrews they had to decide what to do about the throne. They knew how things worked. If it were left vacant for long someone one would try to take it.

Tayler asked Andrews, "How long before the king can climb back on the throne"?

Andrews, "If things keep going well, a month".

Lance, "That is too long to leave it open".

Zorn spoke up and said, "If I and Alfred and Lance and a dozen of your soldiers went to Wexford". "Who would doubt that I was king".

Lance, "It is not legal, but I think it would work".

It was not popular, but they agreed to do it and agreed to leave in three or four days if Andrews said O.K.

Lance and Alfred would ride horses, the soldiers would be on foot, and Zorn would be in the jeep ambulance. Marvin's men had painted it green and brown camouflage because red crosses did not mean anything at this time. Then Andrews appealed to Tayler that she should go in case any of Zorn's wounds opened, and there were several. When Tayler asked her about the king, she told him the king had Ramones and the nurses. Tayler relented and told her to ride in the jeep.

In the meeting Zorn had asked one question that surprised Lance, he had asked if the men would take some of those things, they threw that killed people. They had at least 3 days to get ready. Lance let Mills pick out the soldiers to send. Then he went and talked to Lt. Marvin.

Each soldier carried his weapon and two full 30 round clips and a grenade hanging on their vest. There would be more ammo in the jeep along with the doctor's bag and equipment.

One other thing was a Looper also known as an M-79. Lance did not like parting with Gwen Grey, but he felt this was necessary. Three days later After a good early breakfast, they started. Major Mills drove the jeep and just limped along with his men. It was early afternoon when they arrived, and Erick and Taggard met them. They were overjoyed to see Zorn on his feet and healing. Over a dozen people gathered around Alfred to welcome him back. Zorn was to act like the king without saying he was king. The trailer behind the jeep carried the men's Army cots and a tent and they set them up in a corner of the courtyard. The men set up a small tent for Andrews. Lance told Major Mills to have a man on guard duty all night every night. In the room off the main hall Lance, Mills, Zorn, Alfred, Erick and Taggard had a meeting. They talked about the running of the kingdom and Lance asked if they had been any intruders. Erick hesitated and said yes in the south and the west I feel we were being tested. There were no fights supposedly they were just traveling or checking for pastureland, and we let it pass.

Lance, "They would have heard about the king and think it would be a good time to attack". Erick and Taggard agreed, and Zorn told them to have patrols out every day. Later when Lance and Mills were circling the castle checking its defenses Lance told Mills that he believed they would be attacked. Mills, "Then we need to look the hall over really good and plan our fields of fire".

28

Cambridge sends a note

Veer was at the project center, the large conference room had a twenty-four feet long table, but there were more big shots than could sit at it. The three huge corporations, the top people from the project. They were giving reports on what they had done and what they wanted to do. The bottom line though was that no one was having any success. They had succeeded in projecting a few small objects and killed a few rats but that was all. Veer had an idea; "do you think you could send an object back to them?"

Planck spoke for the group and said, "maybe."

Veer, "I know if they can they are trying to repair the device". They agreed on that.

Veer, "Well they may not have the parts they need; can you send them a message asking them what they need"? There was talk around the table with general agreement that they would try. One of corporations talked about a life saver device just large enough for a few people at a time. Some liked the idea, but some said making 100 jumps would lead to disaster.

Veer, spoke up, "Gentlemen please just keep working these people's lives depend on us".

Then Planck spoke, "No gentlemen the whole world as we know it depends on you".

29

Lance and Mills at Wexford

Then it was night and they all got on their army cots, leaving one man up. Each guard would be on duty for four hours, but the night was peaceful. After the basic breakfast, the next morning Lance got with Sgt. Mills and told him send four of your men well-armed in the jeep to base.

Sgt. Mills said, "All right why".

Lance, "Tell them to get the key from Marvin and get that F-150 out of the parking lot and make sure it has gas." "Then have them load up two porta pots and some M R Es and bring both vehicles back". Then Lance and Mills spent over two hours studying the hall. Their M-4s could reach out and touch somebody and the Looper could send a grenade out 350 yards.

The two vehicles made it back in the afternoon, unloaded their cargo and set them up. The M R Es were only for backup. The hall was large, but it was crude, the open pane less windows gave light in daytime but at night it was dark. Fire pits and smoking torches did not help much. The locals were totally curious about everything. Lance had instructed his people you can explain everything except your weapons. Capt. Andrews reputation as a doctor had become known and she had a steady stream of patients. Early on she and two of the scientists had started making more antibiotics and she was glad they did. They were not out of their original supply, but they were getting low. The castle's water supply was a well and Lance did not really trust it. Tomorrow he would send the jeep back for the water trailer. Two of Sgt. Mills soldiers had volunteered to help the Kings cooks and they had helped the food, but they needed spices. All right the jeep could get what Dr. Andrews wanted and spices as well as the water trailer. Taggard came to Lance and told him his patrol had seen six knights in the south but when they rode toward them, they rode away. Sgt. Mills had joined them and said, "that is a bad sign." And added, "they are looking for a weakness." The three of them went to Zorn and told him. Zorn told Taggard to put more patrols out and asked Taggard to send Erick to him. When Erick came Zorn told him to push the peasants to get as much hay and storable food into the compound as possible. Lance asks Zorn if he thought there might be a siege. Zorn responded that it was common to try to starve people out.

Gen. Tayler was in the project building it was buzzing, the had just received a transport. It was only the size of a bar of soap, but it was a transport. Tom Chang was about to open it. Chang opened it and found it contained paper. After he unfolded it, he saw a lot of project formulas and information. What was most important was one line, can you send us a list of what you need to repair the device? There was whooping and hollering.

Tayler asked Chang, "Can you do that?"

Chang, "Not at the moment we have been working on the complete device, I believe we can in a few days."

Tayler, "Great get your people on it". Now Tayler went to the hospital and found the king siting up, it was a great sign. Gen. Tayler phoned Mazak and asked him to come to the hospital. Soon Mazak was there, and Tayler was trying to talk to the king. Tayler called Lance and asked if he could get with Zorn. In a few minutes he was with Zorn and Tayler ask him to put Zorn on the phone. He did and Tayler put the king on his phone and the king was amazed by the phone. Tears of joy ran down the king's face as he talked to his son. Doctor Ramones was there now and told Tayler she though the king could go to Wexford in two weeks if Dr. Andrews was still there. Now Tayler went to see Gwen Grey, she already knew about the transport, and was happy about that. Tayler told her about the king's condition and that was good news. Tayler went to his office and after checking on a few everyday things he called Bradley at Windmere, he did nearly every day. Before Bradley had gone to Windmere Tayler had a scientist make him a solar charger. Bradley told him things were going well, but they kept hearing rumors about a king Offel in the west. Bradley invites him to come and talk to them. They talked about logistics and at the end Bradley told him prince Richard likes Brown.

At Wexford Lance, Mills, and Zorn were out south of the castle where the intruders were usually seen. There were some trees and then a large open area and then a forest. Zorn told them the usually come out of the forest and when we show they go away.

Sgt. Mills, "I have an idea, why don't we send them a message".

Lt. Lance, "All right, how"?

Mills, "It was not for us, it was in transit to Iraq, it just happened to be at our base when we did the jump".

Lance getting irritated, "All right what"?

Mills, "Still in the crate a 50 rifle".

Lance, "We have a sniper rifle"?

Mills, "Yes we do, and we could set him up on that rise and when they show up, we shoot their horses not them so they can take the word back".

Lance, "He might have to wait several days".

Mills, "That would be all right we could put a team there they could rotate".

Zorn, "You can do that"?

Sgt. Mills, "Zorn a M-107 50 CAL. rifle can kill something far away". Two days later they had it set up with a team of three and each one fired two practice rounds. It was four days later that the intruders showed up again. They were now about a half mile away and the team had been told that was as close as they got. Corp. Jones happened to be on the rifle at that moment. He took careful aim and fired and being careful to fire one round at a time fired two more shots. The fourth rider had ridden away. The three knights from the three downed horses had ran into the woods.

Sgt. Mills and Zorn had heard the shots and soon they were there. Zorn found it hard to believe they had killed the horses from that far away. One of the horses had a water bag on its side.

Corp. Jones asked Zorn to watch the water bag and he aimed carefully there was a loud blast and the water bag exploded.

Zorn was speechless he had learned rough English so fast, Andrews said he either had an extremely high I Q or just had an ability with languages.

Mills told the team to move the set up to the top of the hall if one of those archer positions were strong enough, this place had done its job. Sgt. Mills told them after they got it set up on top of the hall that he would add three more to the team and wanted someone on guard all night.

30

Cambridge receives request

Veer was at the project; the place was abuzz. Veer looked up Planck and asked what was going on.

Planck explained that they had got a message back from the group. That is good Veer told him.

But Planck cautioned not all good. "Yes, they sent us a list of parts they need and some of them we do not have."

Veer commented, "but we can make them."

Planck now told him there is a time element. They are being threatened by a king with an army of over one thousand and to defeat him they might have to kill 500 men.

Veer, "Holy crap that could change the world".

Planck, "Yes killing that many men that long ago could eliminate a million descendants."

Veer, "What are you going to do"?

Planck, "We are going to work like hell, because we know our lives depend on it".

31

Tales of war at Fort Sherwood

Two weeks later Lance had sent the Jeep and the F-150 back to the base to get the king. Four armed soldiers in the Jeep two in the back of the truck and four on horseback. They were prepared for trouble but there was none. Two nights earlier two knights had traveled through and told them tales of war. The king with the huge army had just taken over their small kingdom. These two were running away the conflict was for doomed and now they were attacking a small kingdom west of them. Lt. Lance had discussed it and tried to plan what they should do. They knew there was no way this place could stand up to an army like that. They debated, what if they surrendered tried to make a deal. There was a possibility that they might get to stay on the throne, or he might line them up and kill them and put his on people on the throne. They decided they would have to leave it up to the king and Zorn.

They got on the phone to Gen. Tayler and told him all about the situation. Then they asked him the big question, if the king and Zorn wanted to leave the castle and bring the castle people. Could they come to the base?

Tayler told them he would have to talk to others.

Now Lt. lance told Gen. Tayler that Sgt. Mills had a different plan.

Tayler asked him what it was.

And Sgt. Mills on the phone told Gen. Tayler, "this invader is obviously a bad guy, why not let Lt. Marvin and his gunner wipe them out."

Gen. Tayler did not even answer and told them he would call later. Tayler grinned, yes that was the logical answer, if you have a cancer, you cut it out, but you cannot always do the logical thing.

Gen. Tayler got a group together, representing everyone. There was Gwen Grey, scientist, army officers and enlisted, and explained the situation. This powerful king from the west is killing and conquering. We are told he has lined up captives and killed them. We are told he wants to capture this whole area. What are your suggestions?

Chang a scientist asked if they had tried to negotiate.

Tayler answered, "negotiators have been sent, they do not come back."

A Sargent ask, "what does the king and Zorn want to do?"

Tayler answered, "they may want to come here for safety with their castle people, they know they cannot fight this invader."

A scientist said, "that does not solve the problem, they would come after us next."

A corporal spoke up and said, "let the Basterds attack us."

Gwen Grey spoke then saying, "yes, I am sure we could defeat them, but we might have to kill 500 of them."

Azak spoke up then talking about the timeline.

Two other scientists jumped in talking about the timeline.

Capt. Nimmer broke in and asked them, "how much time do we have?" He was told it depended on whether Wexford fought or not, three to five weeks. Nimmer asked Chang, "can we do the jump by then?" Chang answered he did not think it was possible, the present had not jumped the parts yet.

Col. Murphy entered the conversation saying, "it looks like we have a fight on our hands."

Gen. Tayler began to talk about another suggestion. It has been suggested he told them to set up an ambush to halt them and for Lt. Marvin and the helicopter to annihilate them.

A soldier asked about the gatling ammo.

And Col. Murphy answered, "yes it would probably use all of it but what better use."

Roberts, one of the device scientists talked that they were talking about destroying the timeline taking millions of people out of existence.

A soldier asks Roberts if he were suggesting they surrender to the invader, are you asking 376 people to die to save your timeline? Roberts began talking that it was not his timeline, it was the world they had come from, and he hoped for it to be the same when they jumped back. They could not come to a consensus and the meeting broke up. Lt. Marvin had been at the meeting, and he followed Gen. Tayler back to his office.

Lt. Marvin opened, "Gen. Tayler, my gunner and I can do what you talked about".

Gen. Tayler, "I am sure you can, but the group has to decide what it wants to do".

Lt. Marvin took a deep breath and said, "No sir, no one in that room can make that decision. You are the general, in the end you will have to make that decision".

Gen. Tayler said, "Marvin will you go to that footlocker and get a bottle of whiskey"?

Lt. Marvin replied, "Yes sir". At this same time Gen. Tayler was calling Col. Murphy to come to his office. From a desk drawer Tayler got three glasses and poured drinks. When Murphy saw the drinks, he knew there was some serious talking to be done.

32

Bad news at Cambridge

Planck phoned Veer and asked him to come to the project. Veer on the seventh floor of this fancy hotel phoned the room next to his and woke his chauffeur. He told him they had to go to the project. By the time Veer got dressed the chauffer had the limo waiting on him. Veer stayed in the limo until he parked it and then they walked in together. Harold was a lot more to him than just a chauffeur. They went to Planck, and he told Veer that they had received another message. It was not good news; They would be forced to fight a major battle in three to five weeks or surrender.

To Veer this was terrible news and he asked if that was all. Planck told him no, that they were still saying they had to have those parts. Veer reacted angrily telling Planck to send them to them.

Planck told Veer as he had before, we do not have them. These are exceedingly difficult to make, and it takes time.

Veer red faced, "Dam it man they do not have time and we are not just talking about saving them. We are talking about saving the world as we know it".

33

The copter flies at Fort Sherwood

Zorn talking to Lt. Lance, "The king does not want us to fight an army of over a thousand warriors".

Lt. Lance, "What does he want to do"?

Zorn, "The king believes you and your fort can defeat this attacker and he would like to move his family and his castle people into your fort".

Lt. Lance, "I will have to get an answer from Gen. Tayler".

Later at the base Gen. Tayler was having dinner with Lt. Marvin in the common mess hall because he had a job for him.

Gen. Tayler, "Is the chopper fueled up and ready to go"?

Lt. Marvin, "Yes sir".

Gen. Tayler, "Tonight about 8 P. M. full dark I have a mission for you. You are to take us up to 4 or 5 thousand feet and take me west. There is a huge army west of us and I want to know where it is. Just after full dark all their campfires should be lit up and it is a dark night at that altitude, they will not see us".

Lt. Marvin, "Yes sir, I will be ready". It was a few minutes past 8 when Tayler went out to the motor pool. Marvin and his men had pushed the helicopter out of the hanger on its rolling platform. Tayler asks Marvin if he was ready, and Marvin replied yes and began to start the copter. A few minutes later Marvin gave Tayler a thumbs up and motioned for him to get onboard. Tayler climbed in buckled up and put the earphones on. The helicopter lifted smoothly off the platform and began to rise. Marvin circled the base twice gaining altitude and then as Tayler directed flew over Wexford still gaining altitude. Now Tayler asked him to fly due west. They were up to altitude now and they flew about 70 miles west and Tayler did not see what he wanted. Tayler had Marvin fly about 5 miles south and then turn east. And dam there it was campfires all over the place. Probably a 2-mile circle of campfires about 60 miles west southwest of Fort Sherwood and about 40 miles from Wexford. Tayler had Marvin circle it and he took some pictures and they headed back to base.

Back in his office he phoned Lt. Lance and told him where the attacker was.

Lt. Lance wanted to know if they had made any decisions yet.

Gen. Tayler had to tell him no not yet. Tayler went to Gwen Grey's office, and they began to discuss it. Tayler brought up the fact we may be here forever. Part of our decision must face the fact that whatever we do we may be here afterwards.

Gwen Grey agreed with him that their jump may have been a freak thing that they could not be repeated. They talked and talked, and it boiled down to if we do not jump before the attacker gets here, we must fight him.

Gen. Tayler wanted to know how close do we cut it, one day, a week, what.

The next day the studious scientist Roberts came to see Gen. Tayler and was soon telling him he studied English history. That according to history both Wexford and Windmere get defeated.

Gen. Tayler thanked him and told him he would put that into the equation. Tayler cussed under his breath, he was dammed if he did and dammed if he did not.

He made one decision, he called Lt. Lance and told him where the attacker was camped. He then told him that yes, the king and Zorn could take refuge in the base with up to 150 of his people.

Lt. Lance told him that they would be happy to hear that and asked about a timetable.

Gen. Tayler thought about it and told him that he thought they had 7 or 8 days. Then he told Lance to be safe they should be finished in four.

Lt. Lance told him he agreed with him and that he would advise them.

Then Gen. Tayler told him you Dr. Andrews and all our people back here inside 48 hours, that is an order.

Lt. Lance told him yes sir.

Gen. Tayler went and looked up Col. Murphy and told him to have his men to erect that tent city again. Tayler told him for their safety the king of Wexford and his people are coming here. Tayler then went to see Gwen Grey, and he informed her of his decision, and she thanked him. Tayler told her I still do not know about the fight. We know if we do not jump, we must fight, but how close do we cut it.

Now Gwen Grey surprised him by asking, "if the attacker has enough men and they are wild enough or good enough," "could we lose."

Wow Tayler thought before he told her any battle can be lost and over confidence is a bitch.

Again, she surprised him, then if we ambush him even if we did not annihilate him, he would be weaker when he attacked us.

Tayler had to tell her he agreed with her.

She then inquired what he was going to do.

Gen. Tayler then told her, "I will probably do the ambush, but not until he is close. We must give the scientist as much time as we can."

34

At Cambridge push harder

Senator Veer was at a regular weekly meeting and the different corporations were all giving reports. Veer was disgusted, it seemed like little progress was being made. They were having trouble making the parts the base needed because some of the main scientist were at the base. After the meeting broke up Veer went to Planck's office.

Senator Veer, "You know we are running out of time, that rogue king is coming at the base, and I know Gen. Sam Tayler even if he were to lose, he would take hundreds with him".

Planck deflated, "I know what you say is true and I push as hard as I can and offer rewards, but progress is so dam slow".

Senator Veer, "Have you stressed to them what will happen if Mac fights that battle"?

Planck, "I have to all the people at the top".

Senator Veer, "Maybe you should broadcast it to everybody".

35

Sherwood copter attack

Sgt. Mills was talking to Zorn, and asked him how this attacker would be traveling?

Zorn told him, "On horseback like everybody else."

Sgt. Mills then rephrased it that would people be able to tell who the king was.

Zorn then answered, "that yes, they would because the king and his closest knights would have fancy armor and the best horses and some of his knights would have flags on their lances."

Sgt. Mills was working on an idea that he had to present to Tayler. Sgt. Mills now asked Zorn, "if something happened to this king would they still attack."

Zorn could not answer. Zorn added one thing, that this king traveled with his army all around him, that he did not lead them.

Now Sgt. Mills got with Lance and began telling him of a plan. That if they used the helicopter and took out the king the army might go away.

Lt. Lance countered that they might just choose another king and proceed.

Sgt. Mills told him, "Yes, but it would at least slow them down."

The second day was chaotic Capt. Andrews came back to the base and the king and Zorn also.

Grey told Gen. Tayler, "there are 9 or 10 quarters in the science wing that are not being used why do not you put the king and some of his people there?" Gen. Tayler thought it was a good idea and looked up Zorn and took him to that section.

Zorn was pleased but asked for what Tayler called army cots.

Tayler said sure but what for.

Zorn told him to put extra people in some of the rooms and for two guards to sleep outside his father's room.

Sgt. Mills was back and two days later he went to Lt. Marvin and told him of a plan.

Lt. Marvin called Tayler and Lance out, Mills had heard lately that the attacker was close to Wexford. Sgt. Mills wanted to do a surgical strike Lt. Marvin and two riflemen with M-4s all three with night vision. They would try to locate the king's tent and take him out. Reluctantly Gen. Tayler said yes but told Lt. Marvin do not get below 500 feet and that is an order.

Lt. Marvin Crashes

Later it was dark, and everything was ready the night vision the sharpshooters. Gen. Tayler and Lt. Lance watched them load up and the helicopter warm up. Now it eased up and began to skim across the parking lot and then the grass. It was 10 or 15 feet up when suddenly it fell back to earth with a hard landing. Everyone who could find an extinguisher grabbed one and the ran to the helicopter. There was no fire but one of the soldiers was hurt.

Tayler and Lance got Marvin out and asked him," what happened?"

He told them he did not know it had suddenly lost power.

Tayler grilled him that he had told him it was in excellent shape. Marvin answered it was, but my men and I will dam sure find out. Later in Tayler's office they had a what now meeting. Well using the helicopter is out, that hard landing did some damage.

Lance spoke up saying he thought something funny about it. They talked about different plans and what they should do.

Sgt. Mills came in then and told them you might want to come outside, there is a glow in the west.

They went outside and that was in the direction of Wexford. They were sure the attackers were burning Wexford. They talked now that if they did an ambush it would have to be between base and Wexford. They called it a night and went to their quarters.

At 11 o'clock the next morning a greasy Marvin was in Tayler's office. Soon he was telling Tayler that Phitto had a partner, and he was still causing trouble. They had put something in the fuel and clogged the fuel line. Tayler asked him if, he was sure. Marvin called in a sergeant with the clogged fuel line.

Marvin told Tayler you need to have everyone aware of this traitor. Marvin left and Tayler was angry, that was all he needed a troublemaker. Later that afternoon with people he knew he could trust he planned the ambush. That hill where we had trouble before. About forty men all to have horses or hum vs to get away. Rifles and the 107. This is to damage them and retreat. Gareth and Mills can handle that. Lance you and I must plan the defense of the base.

The Sherwood Ambush

They were on the back side of the hill and using shrubbery for cover they were looking at the invader's army. Yes at least a thousand half on horses' swords, lances, pikes, war axes and a whole lot of archers. Col. Murphy hollered, "check your weapons." Then he hollered, "Jones you ready with the 107?" He got a roger on that and said, "men when Jones fires everybody fires."

Jones fires the 107 and a knight falls off his horse. Now all around him rifles are firing, and more riders fall off. Horses fall, footmen are falling over. A small group of knights tries to charge the firing rifles and are decimated. Many archers try to reach them, but they do not have the range. They are in full retreat now and Col. Murphy hollers, "cease fire." Now Sgt. Mills tells them to pack up and get back to base. Now Gen. Tayler is having a pow wow and asked them, "how many did you kill." Col. Murphy answered and told him that they estimate they killed about ninety.

Sgt. Mills added that the enemy retreated very quick, or they would have killed more. Lt. Lance then questioned them about them continuing to attack. Col. Murphy began explaining that this was not a normal situation, there was nothing to judge by.

36

Confusion at Cambridge

Planck called Veer and told him he needed to be at the project. Within 45 minutes Veer was in Planck's office. Quickly Planck got into it, there has been an earthquake in the timeline.

Veer quizzes him about what he thinks happened.

I do not know but I would guess that people died, that has a large effect on the timeline. When people die at the wrong time.

Veer quizzed him about when can we do the jump?

Planck put him off telling him they were not ready yet.

There was a large gathering in the conference room. The large bump in the timeline was the main topic. All the major entities had representatives there. There was arguing and things went back and forth. A short break was called, and Veer stepped outside for a breath of fresh air.

He was surprised when Lillian Georgette joined him. Georgette was number two under Planck.

Georgette tells him I know your daughter is back there and most of the people agree something big is about to happen. Planck wants to do more test; I am willing to do it now.

Veer pointed to the conference room and asked her do you have the votes to override him?

Georgette said, "Not at this time."

37

War at Fort Sherwood

At the base Gen. Tayler and Lance were checking and rechecking. Col. Murphy and Sgt. Mills were assigning positions, rechecking fields of fire and the lights they had placed around the berm. Now they heard noise, the sounds of horns, cartwheels, the clank of armor, and the sounds of horses. It was obvious by the sounds they were surrounding the base, but they were staying in the forest. They waited and it was tedious, and two hours went by and now from the forest on the west side of the base swarms of arrows came into the fort. Tayler's men did not have shields and two were hit.

Quickly Col. Murphy hollered, "Clark and Ferguson put grenades in that Forest." Soon they were hearing a dozen grenades explode. They heard screams and the arrows stopped. The base because it was a high-risk base had light poles all around the base on the inside of the berm Now Tayler went to see Lt. Marvin who was working on a secret project. The base for some reason had two halftracks, on one of them Lt. Marvin was building a tower with an arrow proof compartment on top, with two gunports. It had a one-inch Plexiglas window in front and could hold two men if they were friendly. It could be driven anywhere around the perimeter. The prince had told him that since the berm was only dirt the attackers would try to tunnel through it. The men in the tower could see over the berm and shoot anyone trying to tunnel through.

Gen. Tayler asked Lt. Marvin, "does it have lights."

Lt. Marvin said yes, "two and two backups." Just then Tayler's phone buzzes, they have their own cell phone tower. Gen. Tayler is told there are arrows coming in from the east side.

Can you see the archers?

No but we see the area they are coming from.

Have Jones use his looper and put a few grenades into that area. Two minutes later they hear distant whomp whoop, whump.

Jones calls says he heard screams, no arrows right now.

Now mills at the main gate calls and says there is a large group of men with a large log, they are going to try to tear down our gate. Sam says, "blast them with your M-4s," now they hear the rapid fire of the M-4s. the attackers seem to have forgotten that they are not attacking a solid wooden door. This was an iron gate that the troops could shoot through.

The phone buzzes again and Mills said 20 dead or dying 2 or 3 got away. They are sending women up to get the dead.

Sam said, "let them if they do not try anything." The bodies were all gone now but the log remained. Now another group of twenty men ran up to the log raised it up and tried to ram with it. Mills men ripped them apart with their M-4s and now there were 20 more dead and dying.

Gen. Tayler's busy phone buzzes and Lt. Gareth says, "they are messing with the berm on the east side."

Gen. Tayler asked Marvin, "can you take the tower to the east side?"

"Yes," Lt. Marvin said, "Bill and I will ride in the tower Harry can drive." In twenty minutes, Marvin called and said they were in position.

Gen. Tayler asked, "what do you see?"

Lt. Marvin replied, "men digging."

Tayler simply said, "kill them."

Marvin and Bill started shooting the diggers, and now they are saying, "we are getting arrows."

Tayler asked, "are they piercing the booth?"

"No" Marvin said, "we killed 12 before they quit trying to tunnel. Now the site is empty."

Tayler says, "all right you probably need to stay there for a while and then go back to the motor pool." Now Tayler gets word that there are people on the west side, lots and lots of people. Tayler said, "get the machine guns and loopers over there they may try to conquer the berm with just sheer numbers." Tayler to Lt. Marvin, "get the tower to the west side they are going to attack the berm in mass. Get anything we can spare over there." Ramos has the 50 on top of the water tank, that is a good spot. Now they heard horns and drums and Gen. Tayler said, "get ready it is about to start." Suddenly there was a mass of armed men, they rushed seven ladders to the berm to give them traction. Soon there was a huge cacophony of 50s, 30s, loopers, and M-4s, a few got over the berm and died on the inside. They estimated 250 had died before they retreated. Tayler sent armed men to push the inside bodies out over the berm. Now all was quiet even the birds were quiet. Tayler got still another call; A fireball had just come into the base. They must have a catapult; "Can you locate it?"

It is in the west, unroll the fire hoses and get them ready. Lt. Marvin takes the tower with a looper to the west side.

Soon after he got to the west side Marvin said, "I just saw a fireball come in." "It came from about 300 yards west of the berm."

Tayler said, "have Ramos use the looper and walk the grenades through their position."

Ramos reply, "yes sir" and soon they again heard the whomps of the grenades and the fireballs stopped. They waited tensely for the next hour and nothing happened, and it got dark, and all the bright pole lights came on. That night nothing happened, but from the noise and campfires they knew something was in progress.

The next morning in the tower Marvin said, "what the hell is that?" Gen. Tayler asked, "what does it look like?"

It looks like a Roman turtle about 10 feet wide and 5 feet tall and each segment about 20 feet long. They are walking the first segment up to the berm. They are going to use it to tunnel.

Mac said, "if that turtle wood is as thick as my guess M-4s will not do." Tayler to Ross, "stir up at least a dozen Molotov cocktails and take them to Marvin." An hour later they start tossing the Molotov's over the berm. Soon they could see fire and smoke, the turtle was burning.

Marvin to Tayler, "I think I have located where their big cheeses are." Gen. Tayler says, "Well get with Ramos and the 50 and wipe it."

38

An A-bomb at Cambridge

The phone rang in Veer's hotel room. It was the project manager, Veer, "we have problems, come down to the project." Veer did not object because he could tell by Planck's voice that this problem was worse than usual.

Veer phoned his driver in the hotel room next to his. Harold said, "what's up senator?"

Veer told him they had to get down to the project. Soon they were pulling up to the shiny new building. They were shocked not to see their regular two Rent a Cop, but approximately 20 soldiers in full military gear.

Planck came out to assure the troops that Veer, and his driver were supposed to be there. Planck took them inside and began to explain what was going on. You know of course that two weeks ago we had to tell the world about the time quakes and how they were changing history.

"Yes, yes," Veer said, exasperated.

"Well," Planck said, "it is a hell of a lot worse now, we are getting a time quake every few minutes. The names of countries are changing, the borders of countries are changing. Three different countries have had major ethnic shifts." That has been happening before. "Well now," Planck said, "the U N is in its emergency session, two hours ago they gave us an ultimatum."

Veer asked, "what kind?"

To answer Planck took them into the next room. Four soldiers were in it, an aluminum box about twice the size of a footlocker sat in the middle of the room.

Veer looked at it and asked, "what is in it?"

Planck answered, "a little over six pounds of Plutonium."

Veer replied, "you are joking."

No, the U. N. has given us that ultimatum that we either get them back or destroy them.

Veer, "and what if we do not?"

Planck, "the world will be at war with us." They say within 12 hours after the deadline two of our major cities will be bombed. we have 22 hours left to either get them back or stop the time quakes.

Veer, "you are telling me we may have to kill my daughter."

Planck replied, "they are telling us to save the world."

Veer asked, "are they trying to make a jump."

Planck said, "everyone is here doing everything they can."

Veer and his driver sat at the project's small coffee shop. The old waitress was friendly but had no idea of what was happening. Terribly frustrated Veer went into the project with all its electronics, strange devices, memory banks. So many things that he had no idea what they were. He asked what one large device was and was told it was a Heisenberg compensator. Veer saw the lead people in a huddle and went to it.

Planck turned to Veer and said, "we have a problem."

Veer asked, "what is the problem."

One of the other scientists answered saying the device as it is built today needs four times the amount electricity as we have.

Veer asked, "is it available."

A scientist speaks up and says it is out there, but we cannot have it. We would have to shut down the state.

Veer said, "I will call the president, someone else call the governor." It had taken many hours with hollering and cussing to make the arrangements but now they were about to try a jump. Veer watched Planck give the go signal and there were strange sounds and then a brilliant flash out of one device.

Now Planck and others were shouting shut it down, shut it down. Now they were saying get it repaired. Veer went outside and called the president again. He told him about the failed test and asked what if neither option works.

The president says, "I am told the war starts anyway."

39

It's over at Fort Sherwood

In the base, Gen. Tayler says, "they seem to be leaving."

Srg. Mills says, "maybe they are and maybe not." In the late afternoon Gen. Tayler phones Lt. Marvin and ask if the chopper is ready.

Marvin says, "it is not perfect, but it will fly. That hard landing put some wrinkles in it."

Tayler says, "I will be right down I want to see what is going on." As Tayler gets to the motor pool, they are pushing the chopper out on its rolling platform.

Lt. Marvin says, "I will test it first and climbs in." Soon the rotor is turning, and the noise increases, and the chopper rises into the air. Marvin zooms it around the base and now sits it back down. Tayler climbs in and buckles up. The chopper rises into the air. Tayler first has Marvin do a tight circle around the base and then a large circle. It is obvious the attackers have left or are leaving. All they are leaving behind is several large piles of striped bodies. Tayler had Marvin fly up by Wexford and it was burnt, but there were people already working the land. So now they go back and land at the motor pool. A lot of people are there waiting for news including the prince and the king. Tayler tells them, "they are gone; you can go back to Wexford."

The prince came to Tayler and thanked him for his hospitality and said they would be leaving as soon as possible.

Gen. Tayler calls his officers to the mess hall and soon they are giving each other results.

Medical told them, "six people were hit by arrows, and two of them died."

Sgt. Mills reported on how much of their ammo they had used.

Cookie reported on how much of their food stores had been used up feeding the king and his people. They discuss possible sources of food.

Medical brings up the bodies, and that it was dangerous Healthwise just to let them rot.

Lt. Marvin said, "it would be even more dangerous to try to bury them."

Gwen spoke up, "and thanked everyone for doing their jobs well done."

40

One more try at Cambridge

Senator Veer stalks around the project. They do not dare tell him to leave. He wants his daughter back and if they cannot make this thing work, she is going to die. The device had failed three times and the project people were getting desperate. They were running out of time.

The governor, "was hollering that he had to turn the power back on." 99 percent of the state was without electricity. They were at the two-hour window that they were supposed to reserve for the bomb. They were not trying to send the bomb; they were trying one more time to do the jump. The countdown had started 20, 19, 18, 17, 16,

41

Timequake at fort Sherwood

The fort had a peaceful night and now Tayler, Gwen, Lance, and Mills were at the main gate, 20 minutes ago they had just watched the last of the kings people leave. Suddenly, the air was charged with electricity and the ground was shaking, there is fog in the air. It was like an earthquake, but now after a few minutes everything was calm. Lt. Lance was the first to focus on the noise overhead.

He said, "those are English biplanes."

Gen. Tayler said, "yes, and they are circling us." They waved at the biplanes as they circled the base three times then flew away. The fog had gone away, and they looked out through the gate and were surprised to see a paved road. Now they heard sirens, old fashioned sirens, they were coming toward them, so they waited. 30 minutes later ten old army trucks loaded with soldiers pulled up outside the berm, and their officers spread them out. There were four officers, and they were staring at them. They had that frightened look like they were seeing men from Mars.

One step forward with his Webley revolver drawn and asked, "do you speak English."

Lance was tempted to say something cute, but he did not, he simply said, "yes, we do."

With his revolver still pointed at Tayler the officer asked, "who are you and where are you from."

Gwen step forward thinking a female presence might help and said, "we are English and American scientist." She then asked, "can we talk to some of your leading scientist."

The officer with the drawn gun backs up to the others and they talk.

A different officer steps forward and says, "why should we, and how do we know you are peaceful." Our pilots said this was an army base. Lance went quickly to his quarters and got his tablet; he was a collector of historical pictures.

He brought it to the gate and letting them see it through the gate he showed them a whole series of pictures and they were amazed by the device.

Gwen spoke then and said, "we have many things to show your scientist."

The officers talked among themselves and then two of them went to a truck and it rumbled away.

One of the remaining officers came forward and said, "they went to talk to our leaders; this will take a while."

Tayler thought to himself that is very English. The English officers backed up to their troops, and Tayler and his people backed up.

Lance said, "what the hell can we tell them."

Gwen said, "we tell them we know things that can help them in farming and manufacturing."

A sergeant from among the troops comes up to the officers and talks to them and then comes up to the gate. Obviously talking to Sam's troops, said, "can I see one of your rifles?"

Tayler nodded to Mills and said yes with an empty clip. Mills unloaded his M-4 and handed it through the gate. The English sergeant took it to his troops, and they ganged around it.

After a while, the English sergeant brought it back to Mills and said, "will you show us how it works?"

Tayler nodded yes and Mills said, "I will shoot it into the air, but it will make a lot of noise. You must tell your troops that this is a demonstration."

The sarge went back to his people and talk to them, and now an officer said, "you may proceed." Mills had the rifle with a full clip and more on his belt he pointed the M-4 at the sky and in 45 seconds fired 30 rounds, the natives were impressed. Sam had Mills men go to the mess hall and bring out the folding chairs, he wanted this to be as amicable as possible.

Gwen then had them go back and bring ten for the English and the handed them through the iron gate.

Now Tayler talking to Lance and Gwen ask, "if this really is 1919 who do we tell them we are? Time travelers?"

Mills hearing this says, "oh yes, the people of 1919 are not going to believe in time travelers. What else can we do."

Lance says, "if they forcibly take over the base, they are going to find a lot of things they cannot explain."

Gwen says, "what if we convince their scientist just to leave us alone?"

Tayler replied, "I do not think they will do that."

Lance said, "what if we convince them that we can really help them?" Tayler says, "then we would be changing time a lot."

Lance asked, "how long can we run the reactor on just Berm Lake?" Tayler said, "since we enlarged it and filled it full maybe two weeks." To their surprise after so many troops had surrounded the berm, three antique sedans drive up and scientist and a general emerge.

Tayler secretly uses his phone to call the five scientist he had chosen earlier to come to the gate. They arrived and the British scientist began to asked questions and write a lot of the answers down. The general comes to the gate and beckons Tayler to come to him. Tayler and the general start to make some basic agreements. The general leaves after an hour.

After three hours the British scientist asked if they could come back the next day.

Of course, Tayler says yes.

Fort Sherwood 1919

The British sets up tents on all sides of the berm. It seems to be a peaceful custody and Tayler has turned off the pole lights so as not to flaunt diode technology. The next morning the British bring out a large quality tent and set it up for people to meet in. That day there was a military man in the British scientist group, and he asked many questions about the M-4. He asked other military questions too. They try to answer truthfully but there are some questions they do not answer. The scientists are asking real questions and Tayler's scientist know they are filling in blanks. Sometimes they get denial or disbelief like when tectonics came up and the British scientist got a real laugh about the continents moving around. Several things about astronomy did not fit their beliefs, They were sure there were nine planets. The British scientist leave, and Tayler and his crew go to the mess hall.

42

Trouble at Windmere

A messenger that had been sent to Fort Sherwood came to Bradley and said, I have some terrible news for you.

Bradley asked, what is it?

The messenger said, it must have been a wizard.

Bradley, tell me what you mean.

The messenger blurts out, a wizard has made your fort disappear.

Bradley is shocked, he thinks someone made it jump. He knows he is at Windmere forever. He then thinks of Brown, poor Brown. He asked the messenger to take him to prince Richard. The messenger does and Bradley says, I have some bad news for Brown.

Prince Richard quickly says, I will go with you. They find her and Bradley tells her, and Brown begins to cry. She says I will never see my family again. Prince Richard puts his arms around her and tells her he will take care of her.

43

Bombed at Fort Sherwood 1919

A scientist comes up to Tayler and says, "we have another problem."

Tayler exasperated said, "what now?"

The scientist says, "residual radiation."

Tayler answers, "how could we have that."

The scientist said, "simple someone set off an atomic bomb at the time and place we were."

Tayler's crew were shocked, "are you sure?"

"We are positive, where we are now is about two- and one-half miles from where we were."

Lance asked, "you have checked all this."

"Yes, at our time and place there was an air blast, a few hundred years ago." The scientist added our present location is approximately two- and one-half miles east of our previous location. The whole crew was speculating, why would a bomb have exploded there in the past?

Lance said, "it appears to have been at our exact time and location. If it was at our exact time and location, then it was planned and on purpose and our on people must have been a party to it." Some resisted the speculation.

Gwen asked, "why would they do it?"

Scientist Trang, "we must have been harming the future and they decided to stop us."

Then Gwen said, "then they would do that?"

Scientist Trang says, "what we do here has many multiple effects as time goes by."

Tayler spoke up and said, "that is all moot right now. What we must work on is how do we exist here. They say they will give us the water supply and food and we give them scientific knowledge. But we must be prisoners inside the berm."

Someone asked, "for how long?" The British government says we must be secret and stay secret. They do not want their people to know we are time travelers. The British had set up a large quality tent outside the gate and that is where they met the scientist and the people in charge. The base scientists were careful how they introduce themselves. They did not say nuclear physicist, or quantum theory expert.

Tayler went to the scientist meeting and told them, "this is good, but I need to have more meetings with the general."

Gwen came to Tayler, and he saw she was choked up with tears in her eyes and he asked what is the matter?

Gwen said, "I just realized we lost Brown and Sam Bradley at Windmere."

Tayler said, "I know but we had no choice. We did not know the jump was going to happen."

Fort Sherwood Scientist Meeting 1919

The next day at 10 A.M. Tayler, Gwen and Lance were permitted to go out to the large tent to meet officials. They were told their names but not their offices. They seem to be people with authority, one agrees to have people there tomorrow with equipment to start the water supply project.

Another agreed that the next day fruit, vegetables, and meat would be delivered. At 2 P.M. the scientist met, and Tayler's scientist were as honest as possible. There were some things they could not tell them.

They knew now they could not afford to change history. They had found out that this was September 16, 1919.

The English scientist asked a lot of industrial questions, a lot in the electrical field. The scientist meeting ended at 5 P.M. and back inside the group had a meeting with Tayler, Lance and Gwen to discuss the meeting and what they were asking. The next day food arrived, and Cookie was happy with it. Major Philon was pleased with the start of work on the water supply. A river was farther away now but the construction crew said it would not be a problem.

Later in quarters Lance was in Gwen's room, he had gotten tired of the rules, and they were close again. They had been discussing the situation the base was in, but now Lance stood up to go.

Gwen hugged him and then on impulse Lance kissed her and it turned into two deep kisses and then Lance says oh god, I have missed you.

Gwen replied, Oh Lance I am sorry I have missed you too.

Lance says that is all in the past, we must work on the future.

Gwen asked what is our future?

Lance smiled it might be amazing. They kissed again before he left, and he clung to her. Now as Lance walks down the hall, he feels better than he has in a long time. He went to his room to sleep because he had to be at both meetings tomorrow. The technical one in the morning and the scientist one in the afternoon. A name on the afternoon list was awfully familiar to him but he could not place it, a mister Herbert G Wells. The morning meeting went well and in the afternoon meeting there were so many questions, and many they had to dodge. Like how does your base make its electricity? They again asked about their water needs and the scientist put the answer off. Mr. Wells got Lance cornered and asked him a lot of questions. Some Lance could answer but some he had to hedge on because some were on point. When it was over, he went to the scientist club in the barracks building and called Gwen. He had her a drink ready when she arrived.

She said I have been at the device.

Yes, Lance said.

Well Gwen said if you remember one time, we sent back a piece of paper in a small box.

I remember Lance said.

Well I want them to try it again. If it was the project that sent the bomb back, they may think we are all dead.

What would you send them?

I would not tell them when we are, I would probably tell them, dad I am alive.

44

A Surprise at Cambridge

Veer was devastated, his only child was dead. He had been a widower a long time now he was alone. The project was going to have a large memorial service and he was required to be there. His driver had insisted he go. It had been terrible, all those people dead. The U.N. was trying to make the world adjust to the changes but there was a lot of anger and hostility. Leaving the memorial service Veer told his driver, drive.

The driver asked, "where?"

Veer replied, "please just drive."

A week later Senator Veer was in congress, and everyone was raising hell. They all knew he had been the main sponsor of project Camel Otter and he was catching hell for it. He answered their questions and took their abuse. Nothing could be worse than killing your own daughter. Veer's phone buzzed, and he looked at the name. It was Planck, he pushed the no button. The third time Planck called back Veer answered it. "What do you want?"

Planck said, "you need to come to the project."

Veer replied, "that is the last place I need to be."

Planck replied, "for your own good you must come to the project."

Veer said, "I do not like this."

Planck replied, "I know just come."

Veer wondered what the hell could he do at the project? He was trying to mend fences here in D.C. Soon he left congress, and his driver headed north. Three hours later he arrived at the project.

Within ten minutes he was talking to Planck, "dam it you better have something important to tell me."

"I do he said, there are still being changes in time. These changes are totally different. People are not disappearing, but businesses are."

Veer asked, "what do you mean?"

Planck said, "we are seeing industry in England get much stronger after World War one and that did not happen."

Veer asked, "what do you think is doing it."

Plank, "we are not sure, but we think we know." Planck handed Veer a small, folded piece of paper saying we received this a week after we did the bomb.

Veer unfolded it and read the few words; Father I am alive. Veer collapse crying to the floor, "why didn't you tell me on the phone?" Planck said, "I did not think you would believe me."

The 70-year-old Veer regained his composure and Planck helped him up. Veer standing up now and drying his eyes with a tissue said, "what happened."

"Well" Planck said, "we think the last time we tried to jump them it sort of worked."

Veer asked, "what do you mean?"

Planck said, "we think it jump them to right after World War 1."

Veer asked, "how could they be there and not be in the history books."

Planck replied, "we are not sure, but they are not in the history books or the newspapers."

Veer asked, "how can that be?"

We do not know unless they put them in something like an Area 51. Some of H.G.s writing hinted at it but that is all.

45

Elements at Fort Sherwood 1919

Lance came into Tayler's office and said, "the water is flowing."

"Great," Tayler said, "that is a worry off my mind."

"Yes," Lance said, "and we are going to fill the berm lake to the brim." Now lance said, "so you are serious about making a jump."

"Yes," Tayler said, if possible, "we must get back to our own time."

Are the British giving us what we asked for?

"Yes and no," Tayler said, "they claim they are giving us what they have. They claim some of the elements we asked for are not being mined at this time."

"Hey" lance said, "we know where those mines are going to be, we could send a team there to get some. And of course, we would turn it over to the English."

Tayler said, "when those scientists come tomorrow tell them we want to send three teams to secure minerals and they can send as many escorts as they want."

Lance asked, "are our scientist really working now."

Tayler replied, "yes for a change they seem to be working hard." The next night when Tayler and Lance met in the mess hall, Tayler ask, "did they go for it?"

Lance replied, "heck yes, they went for it. When I told them, we knew where to find those minerals and that we would give them the locations heck yes. They said they would have it set up and fake pass ports for our 12 people."

46

Changes at Cambridge

Veer was back at the project, Planck had insisted, saying a different group of scientists have come to me and you need to hear what they are saying. Now veer and his driver are walking in.

Planck greets them and guides them to a conference room. It already has a screen and charts set up and there are eleven people. They are introduced, a lot of double P.H.D.s and then one by one they go to a chart or screen and explain it. One of the charts is an airplane with just one wing and very streamlined. One of the scientists saw Veer look at it and said, the English say they are building that and say they have proof it will work. That Rolls Royce is building a brand-new V-12 for it. And it is whispered that they are working on an aircraft engine that does not have a propeller.

Now veer spoke up and said you are saying that Brittan doing good in industry is a bad thing.

One of the scientists spoke up and said, in itself no. But things have a domino effect. After World War 1 Brittan was in bad shape, and it did not improve much over the years. That was the main reason Hitler thought he could defeat them easily. What if he sees them as a strong powerful nation? He might not attack them. And since they are an ally of France, he might not attack France.

Veer spoke up and said would that not be a good thing?

Two of their scientists spoke up at once and said it might be, but it would totally rewrite world history and we are not the ones to do that.

Another scientist spoke up and said we have seen the effects of people dying that were not supposed to die. We have no idea what the effect that 16 million not dying would cause.it might cause famine, water shortage, diseases, and over population.

After another 30 minutes of sometimes loud talk, Veer spoke up and asked, what do you want to do.

Planck spoke for them and said they want to locate them and try another jump. Veer said that is alright with me just be careful.

47

A Few days later at Fort Sherwood 1919

Tayler watched the three teams of four and each team with their 12 escorts. And besides each man's large backpack, each team had three footlockers on wheels full of equipment. They were traveling on trains and ships to get to the mine's locations. Their escorts had bags of coins to pay locals to dig and dig. Later that afternoon Tayler watched Gwen and Lance leave the mess hall together and even though Tayler had once had a thing for Gwen nothing had ever came of it. Tayler was glad they were happy. Tayler saw Captain Andrews at an empty table with a cup of coffee and a long face. Tayler went over to her and asked, "may I join you?"

"Of course," she said.

Tayler sat down in a chair across from her and asked the obvious, "miss him?" Tayler did not have to name him.

Andrews said, "oh yes Tayler he was so special. To fight those vicious fights and still be so gentle."

"I know," Tayler said, "but we had no part in the jumps timing."

Andrews said, "oh Tayler I am not blaming you, but a girl has a right to be sad when she loses a beau," and smiled at Tayler.

He reached out and touched her cheek and said, "you are a wonderful woman." And he remembered a rainy afternoon a long time ago.

Tayler wondered would things ever be simple again; life was so complicated now. The project had tried to kill them, could he trust them now or would they try to destroy them again. He knew they were just trying to survive too but sometimes they were at cross purposes.

Lt. Marvin came into Tayler's office, "sir we have got the chopper fully repaired."

Tayler said, "that is great thank you."

Marvin asked, "do we have any idea who sabotaged it?"

Tayler said, "yes, we know it was Stenger, and he has wanted private talks with the British. We know but we have no proof. They are still among us. At least two." Tayler, we cannot let the British know about the copter.

I know Marvin said, they were not invented until later.

Tayler said, keep it ready we have no idea what is going to happen.

4 Weeks later at Fort Sherwood 1919

All that had went on in England in the past months, had aroused some peoples suspicion since they were not in on it. It went so far that England's secret service sent a team out to Fort Sherwood. They had a plane come out and photograph it. They came out to Fort Sherwood and challenged the army. The army told them they needed a lot more authorization. They vowed to come back and left.

Tayler and Lance went to Gwen and persuaded her to go to her scientist and talk to them.

She was to ask them if they could make even a small jump.

The scientist agreed to do everything they could. The rare earth teams had returned, and the ore had been received from the refiners. Tayler was sweating, he knew that if the English had to go public with them, they would be scattered. Put in 50 different places, and never get to make the jump back home. Tayler had to keep everyone in the fort to get them back home. They had lost Brown and Bradley; Tayler did not want to lose any more. Tayler went to the gate to keep an appointment with the general. Now talking to the general, Tayler said, we have had a good relationship with you. You have taken care of us, and our scientist have helped your scientist.

The English general said, that is true.

Tayler said, I want to keep all my people inside the fort.

I have understood that the general said.

Tayler said if other people take over, we do not know what will happen.

The general said, we have our own interest. We do not want the country going crazy. We want to learn from you without messing the country up.

48

Send a Note Cambridge from Fort Sherwood 1919

Veer went to the project to see Planck. "Have you found them?"

Planck, "no we have it down to two years, but that is not good enough."

Veer you will keep working on this.

Planck, "oh yes but there is more bad news."

Veer said, "all right, tell me."

Planck, "some way the U.N. found out that we did not blow them up and they are angry. They want us to send another bomb."

Veer, "that is ridicules we kept our word."

Planck, "that is not how they see it."

Veer thought about it and said, "the people that send the notes, can you trust them?"

Planck said, "totally."

Veer took a scrap of paper and wrote a small note.

"It said, to jump you home we need your exact when," Veer.

Veer said, "send that in secret."

Planck said, "of course."

49

English trouble at Sherwood 1919

Lt. Mills was watching the British through the gate. Something was going on. So, mills called Tayler and said, "something is going on with the British. You should be here."

Tayler replied, "I am on the way. Soon Tayler and Lance were both there." There was a crowd out by the large tent, loud talk, finger pointing. After a while one group left. Now the General that Tayler had dealt with came up to the gate. After Tayler joined him, he said, "for now we are still in charge, but I do not know for how long." The English general left, and Tayler and Lance were talking about what he said.

Lance said, "that means we need to do a jump now.

"We do have the refined rare earth elements." Tayler asked.

"Yes, we do," Lance answered.

Have Gwen tell the scientist to have everything else complete, Tayler said.

I will go see her now, Lance said, as he walked toward the offices. The first thing he did on entering her office, was to kiss her. Then he told her what Tayler said.

Gwen agreed and said, yes, we need to jump out of here as soon as possible. The next day the last shipment of refined rare earth elements arrived, but things were very tense. The scientist that came to ask them questions were acting quite different, like they were desperate or in a hurry.

Tom Chang came to Gwen's office; Lance happens to be there. Chang handed Gwen a small, folded note. She opened it and read it, and said, "they want to jump us out of here." She handed the note to Lance.

Lance read it and said, "Gwen they might be wanting to send another bomb."

"My father would not do that," Gwen said.

Lance said, I hate to be the bad guy, but we need to show this to Tayler.

They went to Tayler's office, he read the note, and said, "how can we trust them?"

Gwen, "I trust my father."

Tayler, "Gwen this might not be your father."

Tom Trang said, "there is one more thing, one of our scientist who has ties to England gave them a detailed book on jet engines."

50

Bomb 2 at Cambridge

Veer was terribly upset; he had come to the project to talk to Planck and found the military was there again. Veer found Planck and demanded, "is there another bomb here."

Planck hesitates then says," yes there is."

Veer says, "good god man you already tried to kill them once."

Planck replies, "Veer things are still changing, the whole world wants it stopped."

Veer answers, "so they are willing to kill my daughter."

Planck says, "dam it Veer this is not just your daughter. The world has given us another deadline, 12 noon tomorrow."

Veer says, "so you found out when they are."

Planck answers, "some world scientist did."

Veer asked, "then what are you going to do?"

Planck answers, "we will try our best to jump them, but if it does not happen by 12 noon, we either send the bomb back or the world takes over the project."

Veer says, "I am going to call some people, and storms out."

51

Trying to jump at Sherwood 1919

Tayler to Tom Trang, "are your people ready?"

Trang, "no but they are close."

Tayler says, "call me when they are ready." Tayler calls Lance and tells him to meet him at Gwen's office.

At Gwen's office Lance ask, "how close are they?"

Tayler answers, "less than an hour."

52

At the Camel Otter project Cambridge

Veer was back and demands, "Planck what are you doing?"

Planck answers, "we have run direct power lines from three other nuclear power plants."

Veer ask, "well are you going to use it?"

Planck answers, "it is 30 minutes until the deadline we are going to try to jump them one more time."

Veer watched the people at the different consoles adjust and push buttons and hears Planck say, "now."

53

Timequake at Fort Sherwood 1919

Tayler and Lance were at the gate. Tayler was talking to the English general. The English general had just told Tayler he was out of options, that tomorrow there would be other people coming to deal with them. Suddenly there was electricity in the air. A ground fog formed that filled the whole base. The ground was shaking, the berm next to the gate was collapsing. It was hard to walk, and they could not see the complex, but Tayler and Lance were trying to get to the buildings. The ground continues to rumble and shake. As they got close to the buildings, they see most of them are in terrible shape. Half the mess hall has collapse and crushed some people, three are dead and two have crushed legs. Tayler tries to call Andrews, but his phone does not work. Tayler leaves the wounded to find Andrews or Ramones and Lance goes to find Gwen. Everywhere Tayler goes he finds people either Okay, wounded or dead. The hospital is a wreck, but both Andrews and Ramones seem to be all right and both are doctoring. Andrews asked loudly, Tayler what happened? Tayler had to say I do not know. Tayler told Andrews about the mess hall wounded and went on to see if he could help someone. Soon he came upon two men trying to lift a ceiling beam off a woman. With Tayler's help they did, and Tayler went on. Lance fought his way through tilted walls and fallen ceilings till he got to Gwen's office. Her ceiling had fallen and at first, he did not see her. But now he sees she did like a smart schoolgirl and crawled under her heavy desk. She came out and came to Lance and asked what happened. Lance had to tell her he did not know. Gwen said oh Lance we must go to the lab. Gwen added you know the phones do not work. Lance said I know as they started down the half collapse hallway. Soon they were smelling smoke and then they were feeling heat. When they got to it, they saw fire was raging in the lab. Lance said, you stay here in the hall, I am going to run and back out. Lance did that three times scaring Gwen badly. Now lance held her tight and said there are seven or eight dead people in there, everyone else got out. Now they were aware that someone was spraying water on the lab. They made their way outside and found LT. Marvin and his men had the base firetruck hooked up. The fog was less dense now and the berm that they could see was halfway collapse. In the fog they saw several ghostly figures and when they came closer, they saw, they were scientist that got out of the burning lab. Lance told Gwen you stay here with Marvin; I must go see if I can help. Gwen said I will go to. In the next thirty minutes they went through several bad scenes of dead or wounded people. Now they heard sirens on the outside, a lot of modern sounding and Lance ran to the gate, and the sirens. As Tayler heard a jet fly overhead. Mills was still at the gate and surprisedly the English general and a half a dozen of his troops were too. Tayler told Mills to open the gate and a few minutes later firetrucks and ambulance were arriving. Both drove in through the gate and began doing what they were trained to do. Tayler told Lance take the troops to one side and tell them what just happen to them. Tayler said, I will talk to the general.

54

Phone call at Washington D.C.

Veer's cell phone buzzes and he looks at it. Veer sees it is Planck and does not answer it. A few minutes later Alice his secretary of 25 years comes into his office. She said I think you want to talk to him and left. Veer picked the office phone and said all right what is it Planck? Planck did not hesitate, he said, a very badly damaged, Fort Sherwood has appeared in England, there are no details. Veer said no details. Planck said, none. With tears in his eyes Veer hung the phone up and stumbled out to Alice. Get me on the next plane leaving for London, whatever the airline is, whatever the seat is. Veer buzzed his driver, I am coming to the car, you are taking me to the airport. Two- and one-half hours later Veer is about to board an airplane, he calls Planck and there are still no details. Veer boards the airplane and tells the stewardess as soon as possible bring me a whiskey. The ten-hour flight seemed twice that long, even with four whiskeys he could not relax. His emotions vacillated between elation and sadness. Was everything all right or was his daughter dead or in the past. The plane landed at Heathrow, and he got out of the huge airport as quickly as possible. He went to the cab stand and told them where he wanted to go. The cab dispatcher said, sir that is 60 miles away. Veer said I do not care; I am in a hurry. The dispatcher got him a black London type cab and he was on his way. Nearly two hours later the cab reached Fort Sherwood it was a mess with all kinds of vehicles and equipment. At first, they would not let him enter. He showed them his credentials that he was a U S senator and that his daughter was in there. They relented and Veer walked through the gate. He looked at the crumpled and deformed buildings and thought could she have survived that. Veer studied it, dam what a mess. Tears came to his eyes and blurred his vision. Then with his blurry vision Veer saw someone running toward him. Oh Thank God it was Gwen.

The End

55

Epilogue

They presumed it was conflict between the two jumps that caused all the deaths and damage. No one ever knew for sure. All the equipment was destroyed by the government. 73 people died and 92 were injured. Parts of both those numbers were time travel injuries. Time travel was outlawed worldwide. Sam has retired to a farm in Kansas, Gwen and Lance are engaged. Andrews has a baby boy named ZORN it's godfather is Sam.

Senator Thomas Veer	U. S. Senator
Tom Planck	Over Camel Otter
Gwen Veer Grey	Over base scientist
Gen. Sam Tayler	Base commandant
Lt. Lance	Tayler's right hand
Capt. Dr. Sarah Andrews	Base doctor
Lt. Dr. Ramones	Base doctor
Prince Zorn	Wexford prince
Alfred is Zorn's Brother	Wexford prince
Ann Brown hostage	Windmere hostage
Col. Bradley hostage	Windmere hostage
Lt. Marvin	Helicopter pilot
Capt. Nimmer	Over Reactor crew
Col. Murphy	Over M. P.s
Dr. Phitto	Traitor
Sarg. Mills	Squad leader

LT. Gareth	Troop leader
Timms, Mazak, Smith	Language Experts
Richard	Windmere prince
John River	Windmere Negotiator